The *Flower* and The **HONEYBEE**

Inspirational Talks By

W. NORMAN COOPER

Published by
Truth Center, a Universal Fellowship
6940 Oporto Drive
Los Angeles, California 90069-90291
USA

Distributed by
De Vorss & Company
P O Box 550
Marina Del Rey, California 90291

First Edition

ISBN: O-87516-596-6

Printed in the United States of America

Other Books By the Author

Finding Your Self
Love That Heals
The Ultimate Destination
The Non-thinking Self
Dance With God
Seize The Day

Books About the Author

W. Norman Cooper, A View of a Holy Man
by Roselyn Witt

W. Norman Cooper, A Prophet For Our Time
by Filip Field

CONTENTS

INTRODUCTION

This book is made up of talks which I gave to TRUTH CENTER, a Universal Fellowship, and little effort has been made to revise them for publication.

The talks are reproduced here pretty much as they were presented so that the reader could get a little of the feeling of what it is like to be a student in one of my seminars rather than make them into a literary masterpiece.

I have presented the spiritual Truth in these talks as simply as I could because Truth is very simple and easy to be understood by those who have the humility and childlikeness to look beyond the intellectual reasoning of the human mind. It is my great desire that the reader will find inspiration and help from their simple messages.

The name of the book, **The Flower and the Honeybee,** was borrowed from the title of Chapter XXVII. All spiritual development is dependent upon the inter-relationship between oneself and other entities, much as the flower is dependent upon the bee and the bee on the flower.

In most cases quotations in the book which are from the Bible are from the King James Version; however, in some cases other translations are used when they help to clarify the meaning of the passage.

You will note that I use capitalization in a unique way so that words referring to the Source, commonly called God, are capitalized. Words which refer to the way in which the

Source expresses Itself are not capitalized. When referring to the divine Self, capitalization is used; but when referring to its mortal self, capitalization is not used.

Also you will note that often I use words in a way which is different from their usual usage, including in a few cases, the coining of words to express my meaning.

I want to thank the volunteer workers of Truth Center for their selfless and loving help in preparing the manuscript for publication. I am grateful to those who have read my previous books and have taken time to contact me to tell me how they have been spiritually helped and healed. It is my hope and prayer that this book will also help and comfort many.

Some of the talks included in this book were originally published in Agape, the bimonthly publication of Truth Center, a Universal Fellowship. Should any reader wish to be placed on the Agape mailing list, he or she should drop a note to the address below.

May the love of divine Love inspire the reader as he ponders the following pages.

W. Norman Cooper

6940 Oporto Drive
Los Angeles, California 90068-2639,
USA

The Flower and The HONEYBEE

I

BUILDING YOUR LIBRARY OF WORDS

Words—what are words? Words are not things, they are but symbols—and only symbols—that point to something bigger than words could possibly say. There is no reality in a word although we often think that words are the reality. Words can point to Reality, but words are never Reality.

We need to use words. They are the tools with which we work. In fact, words are the backbone of the art of communication through language. We need to use words for teaching, for sharing, for experiencing—yes—and to express love.

We communicate in the human experience with all the physical senses at one time or another, but we need words to communicate what we feel, what we are experiencing, new truths we have found and for many other reasons. Words are only one of the ways in which we communicate. While I am talking

1

about the spoken word, it would apply equally to the written word.

Words should be used wisely. Meaningless words should be avoided at all costs, yet how much of what we say is actually not necessary. Words can do one of two things. They can either entrap the speaker and the one who hears the word or they can momentarily give a sense of freeing the person who has spoken and the person who hears.

What we have to understand is that the words which one voices may not have the same meaning or nuance to the one who is hearing those same words. For instance, if you use the word love, it's the nuance with which the word love is used; and you communicate the meaning that you mean for that word of love. You may say "I love someone." Or if you think you've had a bad experience in a love relationship, you'll say "Love?"—meaning to belittle the love. The nuance of the same word makes it mean something else. You may say something to someone (that is extremely helpful to you) and find that instead of helping the other person it binds and hinders him.

One time when I was lecturing in England, a lady came up intending to compliment me and said: "My, but you're homely!" Now in America homely means ugly and I thought she was talking about how I looked. I happened to mention this to one who was with me at the time and she said: "That was a compliment. In this part of England homely means that they feel at home with you, that they are comfortable with you."

2

We have to remember that we are not going to get across an exact message through the use of words. Only half of what is said gets across; the other half is what the individual or individuals listening may hear. They will hear from their own experience, their own background, their national heritage, their family heritage and many other things. If one knows that, one is much more tolerant of another. On the other hand if one says: "But I said it! I told him!"—that was only half the message. Was it told in a way that would take care of his needs, his background, his heritage?

Have you ever thought that what your human mind thinks you are—"writes" itself in words? In fact, at the level of the human mind we cannot express ideas without words. We need words, but we must make these words servants instead of masters. How often words become something that are just yelled or screamed out in a sense of anger. The words then are not servants. They have become something that would seem, at least, to be mastering the individual at that moment.

How do you use words? Many of your problems will be because of the words which you use. You may know very well what they mean, but which the other individual who hears those words cannot understand. Does this mean that we stop using words? Of course not. Some people speak too much; others speak too little. Some speak too violently; some speak too softly. In short, we have to cultivate the ability to use words adequately to express what we are feeling at any particular moment.

If you're going to communicate to others you need to be careful about words. Words at best are very difficult to define because there is a dictionary definition and then a perceived meaning to a word. That perceived meaning will come out of your listener's past experience and his present capacity to perceive what you are saying. The great mistake is that we assume that the word itself has a meaning. We often say that a word is in the dictionary and it's defined as such and such a word. But there is much more to communication than just the word, no matter how accurately you use it according to a dictionary definition.

How often people are still using the old words they have used years and years ago. Their whole experience has changed, yet they are using the same slogans, the same trite "truths." How many dead words do you use during a day? Dead words are words that have ceased to have meaning. They have become dead because of the use of slogans. I've known words that in my own time have come into prominence and I've seen them die, such as "Swell!" Don't you remember that twenty years ago people were saying: "It's swell!" Do you ever hear swell have that meaning today? It's more apt to mean bigger, one who is swelling up. Watch that you get rid of any dead words that you have in your vocabulary. They mean nothing to you and they mean even less to the people to whom you are speaking.

You should build a library of words. But once you have built the library of words it will be a continuous building, because as long as you are in this experience you'll be building it. Then be sure that you are using your library, that you can "pull out" as you do when you go to the library and you pull out a book. You'll say: "Read this book, it may help you." You need to learn to pull out the right word, to use the right word.

As long as you are using words it is impossible to have complete unity with another individual. Eventually you must learn to go beyond words to actual feelings. Perhaps you've seen two people talking together, both trying to get their thought across using words. One person would have an entirely different meaning of the words. The other one would answer and he would have a different meaning so that both persons would not understand at all what was being said.

The intended meaning of your word is much more important than the accepted meaning of the word, say, given in a dictionary or in the cultural setting. You must find what your intended meaning is and make it clear enough so that the one listening to you at least gets an approximation of what you are talking about. He will never fully get what you are talking about because he has a different background.

It takes a great deal of spiritual insight, coupled with the proper nuance, to be able to use words so that your meaning will get across —not the meaning that you think you have said. You must be so attuned with the one Word that you will be able to perceive the needs of another; then you won't be spending all your time trying to get your message across.

Some time ago I was interested in a conversation when the question came up about the sunshine we had lately. Several people during that conversation expressed the thought of sunshine in quite different ways. One said: "We haven't had any rain. It's difficult to get along when there's so much sun. I can't go out for my daily walk as much as I would like to." A little later at the same gathering, somebody said: "I hope I have sunshine for my lovely vacation." In the same gathering just a while later, somebody talked about the sunshine and said: "Look at what the sunshine did to me," pointing out that she was using some lotion on her skin so that her clothes wouldn't rub against the sunburn. All three were using one word, sunshine, which had three different meanings.

While I am very fond of words and I enjoy looking up the derivation of words, I have found that the derivations of words are not usually very helpful because words have changed as the centuries have rolled along. What is important is how the word is used today in the culture in which you are operating, the situation in which you find yourself and to whom you are talking. In the art of communication a word which may mean a great deal to you will have little or no meaning to another.

In presenting a teaching or anything else there are really no right and wrong words. They become right or wrong when used. They become right words when they are clearly understood by both the speaker and the listener. They are wrong words when the individual who is speaking the words has no care for the other person and says: "I said what I thought!" You cannot get your message across by merely saying what you think. You have to be so in tune with the Word that your listener gets at least some feeling of what you mean.

Have you ever noticed that you use a different word, a different nuance for a thing that is distasteful to you than you do for a thing that is pleasant or enjoyable? Learn through going to the Spirit and finding that the by-product of that going will be the right use of the right word and the right nuance too.

Above all, it is important that you do not make a teaching into a lot of clichés, slogans and catch-words which should at all costs be avoided. No deep thinker uses clichés, slogans and catch-words. Leave those words to be used by shallow thinkers. What is important is the spiritual meaning, the feeling behind the words, because every word that you have ever spoken has actually two meanings.

An idea which you wish to express such as: "John went to the corner store to buy a loaf of bread" is an actual fact. But there is also another meaning and what that means to the individual who says it. This outward statement: "John went to the corner store to buy a loaf of bread" could also mean "John went to the store to buy a loaf of bread, but I asked him to do it two hours ago." The other person who knows that the family is on relief would probably say: "What right does he have to go and buy a loaf of bread when he's on relief? Can't they get along with what they've got?" The same statement means different things and unless you accept this, you are going to have difficulty, particularly in presenting spiritual Truth.

Words do not really describe the things we are talking about. They describe what we who speak those words imagine what the things are. If you've ever heard two or three people together talking about an individual, you'd think sometimes they were talking about a different individual. It is not the thing said nor the thing heard that is the reality. What "seems to be" is what is thought about the situation—behind the words.

Often I think back to the time when I lectured in Hong Kong and an account of the lecture was handled in three Chinese news-papers. In fact, one of them published the lecture in full. When the time came for printing the name W. Norman Cooper, they had no Chinese words for my name. So when they published the lecture they just made up three different names for W. Norman Cooper. The next day in the newspapers there was an account of this lecture, but does this mean that because they said it was given by someone with another name that there were three

8

W. Norman Coopers? In fact there were four, because there was the W. Norman Cooper who actually gave the lecture.

You may fall for things that are told to you, but anything that is told to you is told out of the experience of the individual who is telling it. You cannot understand the fullness of what another is saying when, for instance, someone comes along and says to you: "My wife is seriously ill." What does that mean? Does it mean that he is asking you to come and visit his wife? Is he needing sympathy? Or is he merely stating the fact? You will, when you hear a statement such as "my wife is seriously ill," form a conclusion as to what the speaker is saying; and it may be quite different than what he is saying. He may be saying "My wife is seriously ill," but implying that "I have a wonderful faith in God and He's taking care of her." Or you can believe just what you think the person means.

Words merely hint at facts, they cannot convey the feeling behind the words. It's impossible for words to convey the feeling. Maybe they can slightly hint at it, but they cannot convey the feeling, because the fact seems closer than the nuance actually is. You must cultivate a constructive sense of doubt. You must always doubt the words that you are saying. And you must doubt that the words you are saying are being understood by the person you are speaking them to.

No words can adequately or fully represent the fact in any situation and we should stop hoping that they will. Don't spend so much time trying to get the words straightened out, but go beyond the words to the Word. Words can never fully be trusted, not even the words given to you by the most inspired Teacher. Just let God's word be interpreted as you so that you become the interpretation.

For spiritual growth you must eventually learn to separate words from the feeling for which the words stand. Words may be a necessary part of the equipment that you need for becoming aware of Truth, but words themselves are never the truth. They are at best but symbols of Truth. In short, words inform about Truth, but they are never Truth Itself. Truth is ever beyond the words spoken about It. Truth is ever beyond the limitations imposed by words, but in our present stage of unfoldment Truth is never obtained without words.

The human experience is the experience of words, the "in part" experience. In the Bible, the writer of   First Corinthians speaks of knowing "in part." Words are "in part." We see "in part," but Truth Itself is Reality—the Whole. Unlike the words which are "in part," Reality, Truth, is the Whole. Words, the "in part," point to the Whole. The Whole is gained when the "in part" words are used and then —and this is the important part—left behind.

The Divine experience is the experience of the Word, the Whole. In the human experience one is constantly moving back and forth trying to find the Word. One should not try to find the Word, but one should live the Word, be the Word, experience the Word. Then the by-product necessary under a certain situation will unfold.

You will never fully understand the divine Power until you rid yourself of the words you use to describe or define God. Let the seed (which Jesus has referred to) die; because as long as you hold on to these words, unless you let them fall away, even words spoken by an inspired Teacher, you will never be completely free. Does this mean you get rid of these words? No, it merely means that you find a new experience by going into the divine Realm.

The Word as spiritual fact is living Reality—Reality Itself being Itself. The word God, Reality, exists now and forever, but you will never fully comprehend God. God is not something that you understand or that you become aware of where He exists. In fact, He exists in no place. He doesn't even exist in your consciousness, really. He is His own Is-ness.

You must be a listener to the Word if you are going to impart to others in words so that they will comprehend Reality. Then the one who really gives the most to the world is not the one who tries to find the right word under a given circumstance, but is listening to the still, small word of Spirit so that he is given the word that is nearest under the circumstances.

11

Sometimes we get into a fight over words. "That's not the right word to express that thought." But words are neither good nor bad. We spend so much time saying: "No, that's the wrong word; this is the right word." Or, "We've got to say it this way because it's not according to a teaching." We go on and on with words, words, words!

Have you ever thought that the Word is the reality behind both goodness and badness? Or what individuals looking on would call goodness and badness? Those looking on who saw Jesus (in what they thought was a fit of anger) whipping the moneychangers out of the temple probably thought this was bad. Was it? Those looking on probably saw it as bad. Again, even the words good and bad can be misunderstood. Misunderstood by whom? By those who hear the ones speaking those words.

Organized religion uses words to define, to explain God, and in that defining and explaining they blind the adherents of their church to its misunderstanding of God. Organized religion is constantly trying to point to God. It does this by using words in which you can believe in God, in Truth, in Reality; but it's all a "belief" in God.

Inspired Religion looks beyond the words to Reality Itself—to the Word. The by-product of that going to the Word will be a more accurate (never a perfect) use of words in our human experience. It will be the best use of words in a given circumstance. Inspired religion is the Word Itself expressed as the

12

spiritual You. Those looking on see you using the right word.

Inspired Religion is always the religion of "in the beginning was the Word." For centuries organized religion has said that the words are necessary for seeking God. But actually God is the Seeker. He is the Source of all action. He is giving you Himself as the Word so that you can be the Word expressing Itself. And the Word becomes flesh so that it can be shared with others.

You must free yourself from all the erroneous words you use, the words that you use rather easily and simply. You say: "All will be well." Will it? That's merely a statement about the human experience. You must realize that you are at-one with the Word. Then you will become the Word made flesh and dwell among others who will hear you. They will think that what they hear is the Word. But what they will be hearing is the by-product, the "Word made flesh" experience.

Words are necessary for spiritual development. But if you are going to really advance spiritually you need to go beyond words to a validity which will be added to your experience. It is the reality of Spirit expressing Itself through you and as You.

The Gospel of John tells us that "In the beginning was the Word...And the Word was made flesh, and dwelt among us." The Word is God; and the Word becomes flesh through each of you as you share the Word.

As you listen to the Word and then impart the Word, you have to do both the listening and the imparting. If you don't you really haven't heard the Word. When you truly listen to the Word, you selflessly impart the Word, and others will be healed, helped, redeemed—yes, and saved.

As "the Word made flesh," you are at this moment the holy instrument by which God shares His greatness, His goodness, His love, His care and His Word with the world.

II

GOD, THE EVER–UNFOLDING OF HIMSELF

With the exception of Buddhism which has no teaching whatsoever regarding God as a creator, all the great religions teach that God is the creator of the universe.

According to the account given in the Biblical Book of Genesis, traditional Christianity places great emphasis on God as Creator. But for genuine spiritual growth a new and more spiritual view of the first chapter of Genesis is urgently needed.

Too often the usual approach to the first chapter of Genesis tends to have its readers humanize their concept of God. They begin to think of God as having characteristics similar to that of a person—a person who expresses thoughts and feelings. If this is what this chapter is attempting to present, the chapter would have to be disregarded, yea, even rejected by serious students of religion.

15

But God, the genuinely creative Principle, is the God of mystery. He is not the God that can be humanly explained. He is the Power which is entirely spiritual. He is forever beyond being described by any story or teaching about Him or His activity; and this includes the first chapter of Genesis.

God cannot be named; He cannot be named even as Creator. He merely exists; He is. He is what the Sciptures declare Him to be —the great I AM, the forever Being, creating anew of His own "isness"—in you as spiritual Reality.

God is wholly spiritual, and being wholly Spirit, He would have to have been above a mere human creation. He could take no part in a human creation or a creation of matter, a material universe. God would have to be a meaningless God if He had spent His time eons ago forming a material creation or a creation of flesh.

If God is wholly spiritual—and He is—we would have to think of Him as creating, not that which is visible, but being Spirit, He would have to create that which is invisible. Then the story in the first chapter of Genesis either purports to tell of a spiritual creation or it is the creation of an outward, visible universe. Which is it?

The God of spirit creates. He has created and is creating only the spiritual world, or if you like, the inner world. He is ever creating Himself and creating Himself

16

anew within and as every living being. When mis-viewed by the ignorance of the human mind, this spiritual creation is thought of as a material creation. But God is that which cannot be adequately conceived of by human intelligence. All that He creates must be seen by the God within each and every one of us. Then the creation in the first chapter of Genesis has to be perceived as an inner creation, a spiritual creation.

God is not a casual Creator who decided to sit down and create a universe composed of a world, moon, stars, fish and whales—and eventually man. His creation is the ever-unfolding of Spirit Itself—of God Himself. That unfolding is the unfolding of each and every living entity.

God is seen in everything—in the world around you, in your fellow humans, in the beauty and even in the ugliness of the universe. God is seen in all and as the ever-creating Principle of all that has reality. But the All in which He is seen is that which the human mind cannot comprehend nor the physical senses recognize.

God has not created you as a mere person and God is not creating you now as a mere person. He is creating you anew, but as God Himself, expressing Himself in you. He is creating you every moment as the complete Nothingness of Himself.

We have to watch the words we use and we have to be very careful when we use that

17

word Nothingness. As I use the word in my teaching, Nothingness is not the opposite of somethingness. Nothingness is Reality which is free from all the limitations of human reason about something. God is not anthropomorphic. He cannot be recognized as some "thing." In the reality of Nothingness, Nothingness is ever unfolding Itself in the realm of the absence of somethingness.

Creation is ever-unfolding, ever-expanding and is an all-inclusive activity. Creation is action, the creative Force. Traditional Christianity would like us to believe that there was a real creation of something in the far distant past; but His creation is the creation which always has existed and always will exist.

His creation is the creation which expresses Itself in and as all living forms including man, including you. His creation is not a creation of some thing; but His creation is the creation of spiritual, absolute Nothingness. This is why the human mind cannot understand spiritual Creation; for the human mind has to have some thing in which to believe, to ponder and sometimes to misunderstand.

"In the beginning God created." In the beginning God is ever creating. What does God create? He creates Himself in the spiritual You. The first chapter of Genesis is full of symbols regarding creation. Unfortunately, too frequently traditional Christianty has taught that the symbols are real. But there was—and there is — spiritual Creation of which the symbols only hint.

"In the beginning was the Word." This teaching of "the beginning" is not what the human mind believes it to be. The question of creation is something we have to face up to because we are so prone to think that we create something. But the Word creates. At any moment God is beginning. Or perhaps more accurately He is continuing his forever creative activity in you and as You.

You, correctly viewed, are the creation of God's beginning.

This "in the beginning" is the ever-unfolding of God Himself, creating Himself in you and as You.

III

DON'T BE AFRAID TO FAIL

So often I've seen individuals who have a talent for something and when they see something else that doesn't fit into their preconceived ideas, they dismiss it. We have to be willing to go beyond even what we believe, beyond what we see, beyond what the human mind tells us is real. We have to be willing to try.

Recently I was watching someone taking part in an activity which he'd never done before. He made some mistakes, but picked himself up and started all over again. I always admire anyone who is willing to try something new.

Be watchful that you don't refuse to do something because you are afraid to fail. So often we don't take on a new activity because we are afraid we are going to fail. But have you ever thought that failure is part of the divine Creation? God creates through failure

20

as often as He creates through what we think of as success, because success and failure are only words.

Do you know the reason we don't try something new? It's because we are afraid of failure. Yet it is in failure that we find success. How many failures did Thomas Edison have before he found the way in which to bring electricity to the world? Failures are the only means of finding success.

God is unfolding Himself and we misinterpret it sometimes as failure and sometimes as success. For instance, was Jesus a failure on the cross? Were the three Hebrew boys failures because they got thrown into the fiery furnace? Or was Daniel a failure because he was in the lion's den?

The great people who have done things for this universe have not been the people who have accepted what they knew to be real. They were willing to go beyond what they knew and in that beyondness they found greatness.

If I were to tell you one thing I would like for you to remember—it would be—don't be afraid to fail.

IV

FINDING THE MYSTERY CALLED GOD

As one studies the great religions—and the not so great religions—he cannot help but be impressed by the vast differences that exist between them. The more one views with appreciation the religions other than one's own, he cannot but be impressed with how much these different religions have in common.

Some religions seem quite primitive, having planted their roots deep in the ancient past. Others have branched off from these ancient religions to form new and helpful (sometimes not so helpful) views of Divinity. Whether the religion is ancient or comparatively modern, there is that desire to help its followers to a more holy view of Divinity.

Some religions preach many gods, but behind this preaching of many gods there is the reality that there is one God, one Principle, which brings harmony and unity to the world. Other religions teach one God, but all too

22

frequently these religions teach their adherents the allegiance to many gods. Whether they realize it or not, these religions also have many gods. They put up with the god of money, the god of indifference, the god of injustice and so on.

While there seems to be this division between many gods and the one God, virtually all religions have one thing in common. That one thing is that there is the divine Law or Principle which is the soul of man and the universe. Religions may give this Law or Principle many different names such as Brahma, Allah, or God, or as some modern religions call it, the Absolute. These are but names and way back behind the name that the various religious groups give to this divine Power is the same governing Law.

All relgions, at least all Genuine Religions, point out that God, the Law, the Absolute must be sought and found, and once found, to become the living Force in the life of the adherent. All religions point up the fact that this great Absolute cannot be understood or recognized by the human mind. That is a statement that could absolutely have been made up to about 150 years ago. Then there was this attempt to manipulate the human mind. But all the truly great religions point up that the Absolute is that which eye cannot see nor the ear hear.

As a word of caution, there can be no such thing as a religion which attempts to unite the human mind with the Divine.

Religion cannot do that. If the human mind, by uplifting and purifying itself could find unity with Divinity, the various teachings would be quite unnecessary.

What is the difficulty in seeking and finding unity among the various religious teachings? Perhaps the greatest of these difficulties is the failure to understand the greatness of the rare soul who views the spirtual universe as the "kingdom" which Christ Jesus said is "not of this world." Individuals fail to realize that all genuinely holy individuals—while living in this world and often not comprehended by even their closest friends and family—call their genuine home the "Realm of the Mystery." That Mystery is God.

Most individuals do not—indeed cannot—recognize that these Holy Ones are those who have chosen to come back as living witnesses to the eternal Truth that there is the Realm of the Mystery called God. These holy individuals appear to all—except those who have spiritual vision—as just ordinary men doing ordinary tasks. But the fact is that being a mystic, living as they do in the Realm of the Mystery, they are no ordinary men. While they should be respected, honored and loved, they are often seen as just another human. Unfortunately, all too often such men are not listened to.

The miracle of God's presence will not be seen in a religious teaching about God, but will rather be seen in the individual who lives the Mystery without consciously drawing attention to his special life. Such individuals are the genuine spiritual Teachers who point the way to unity among religions. Such a one will have respect for all religions and will not fall into the trap of criticizing, condemning or judging religions.

All too frequently individuals get into trouble because they forget to live as they should live — as the genuinely holy Teachers have lived and shown by their own lives. Instead, individuals argue within their organizations — and sometimes with other religions — about the teachings of spiritual Teachers rather than emulating the lives of such spiritual Teachers.

It is — or it appears to be — difficult to travel the path Godward alone. Man finds comfort and compassion — or at least he should find comfort and compassion, although sometimes he finds criticism and condemnation — in the company of fellow travelers.

You may say: "Isn't the human mind capable of tremendous growth?" Yes, but religion must be that which leads its followers into the realm of the "Other," the Realm of Mindlessness, into the Realm of the mind which is free from the conjecture of the human mind. That's what makes it a Religion.

Rules and laws for conduct are necessary for a civilized life, but such rules and laws are not, or should not, be the teachings of any particular religion. These rules and laws (and we have so many of them, particularly now in some of the religious teaching that's being presented to the world) are not of the Absolute, nor are the rules and laws which say that you are to live "this way and not that way." These rules and laws about human conduct are not from the Absolute. The Absolute is of purer eyes than to behold rules and laws of human conduct.

For example, there are rules and laws which say do not murder. The law is practical and necessary for a civilized society; but Inspired Religion says love all, including the murderer. Human law may say to obey the law and for a civilized society this is necessary; but Inspired Religion says to obey the law willingly, not because somebody has written the law or declared it to be the law.

Willingness not enforced by man-made rules and laws is going the second mile of religion. Religions differ as to what these laws should be, but Genuine Religion demands the walking of the second mile. Rules and laws are the first mile. They may enable man to go part way, but Genuine Religion points the way, the second mile—the way to the Mystery which is God. We can obey rules and laws without changing ourselves for the better; but Genuine Religion demands for us to go deeper, to go the second mile, to go to Spirit.

Genuine Religion demands that we seek but never really understand the Mystery which is God. In fact, the difference between a philosophy which says we can understand human action and religion is the fact that Genuine Religion says you cannot understand, that God must remain as He is, a Mystery. Then why do we need religion? Simply because religions are important in man's search for his creative Source.

The present day religion is—or should be —a mutual respect and a great love for all religion. Present day religion needs to look beyond the differences between religions to the one Religion which calls all to recognize, be and live their unity with the mystery of God.

When we find that Mystery, or more accurately when we seek that Mystery, we are walking the path of God-inspired Religion. When we are willing to go beyond man-made rules and laws, which sometimes parade as religious rules and laws, we are walking the path of God-inspired Religion.

Inspired Religion is that which demands of one to go within himself and find the Mystery called God.

V

LIVING AS THE OTHER WORLD OF FAITH

The great need is Faith—and genuine Faith is decision and action. This Faith is not what is so often thought of as faith, because the faith you must have is faith in your divine Selfhood.

Actually, Faith is the paramount necessity in your journey Spiritward. This Faith is not a blind faith or what is called faith in a power separate from one's Self, but Faith is decision put into action.

You can't have a statement of faith or an affirmation of faith, because faith isn't found in words. Genuine Faith isn't an affirmation or belief. Faith is the decision to act spiritually, constructively, because decision and action are part of Faith. It is the decision to act constructively, even though the belief or the knowledge of the human mind does not give its consent to the decision or the action which must follow.

Faith is the decision to act, the decision —freed from human reasoning and human awareness—to face up to the glories of the Other World creation. Faith is the decision to act upon the proclamation by inspired spiritual Teachers—or by one's own Awareness—of the wonder of that Other World "ye know not of."

Faith is not a collective experience; nor is Faith something that is imposed upon you that you must have, such as faith in a teaching, in a group of tenets, a doctrine or dogma, a ritual or even in a Teacher. Faith is individual. You cannot really have genuine faith in another. You must have faith in your Self. But the Self that you must have faith in is your spiritual Self, your true Identity that is ever acting, ever being, ever experiencing—in you and as You.

Do you ever have trouble making decisions? "Should I do this, should I do that, should I do something else?" That's because you believe that you are the fallen man. When we talk about having to make a decision, we are moving back and forth between what is good and bad in the human realm. The fallen man is merely the mortal man who believes in his own belief of good and evil, right and wrong, love and hate. Fallen man is merely a belief in the ability of one's mortal self to do something on its own. But Faith is not something that man can do for himself.

If that is the fallen man, what is the risen man? The risen man is the man of Faith, the man who is acting from Faith and as Faith.

29

The risen man is the God-in-action man. The risen man is the man of decision. He is ever deciding and he is ever acting upon his decisions — decisions which are inspired and controlled by Divinity Itself.

We have to be very careful that we do not feel that this risen man is the object of faith. He is not an object at all. He exists as his own Identity as Faith-in-action. Nothing that God gives is imposed upon man. What God gives is man expressing faith at every moment. If this God could impose any idea upon man, then man could lose that idea at some time. But since these qualities such as Faith are part of man's very existence, he has Faith, he exists as Faith, he is Faith.

Faith is the gift of God to the risen man and in that sense Faith is man's "own," but not in the sense that he has faith and then sometimes loses faith. Faith in the divine Realm is the risen man's "own" gift from God. In that sense he can reject or accept the possibility which Divinity opens to him. At any moment you can accept the possibilities God has for you or you can reject them. One can only become aware of faith as God's gift; but actually you don't become aware of Faith, you are Faith. To put it into language which one can understand, you have to become aware of the fact that faith is the gift of God—He gives you faith.

To have faith is to decide—to decide to act. The decision itself, the act itself, is the gift of God. You can't sit down and decide that you are going to have faith today and that God is taking care of you. You already have Faith and it's only the workings of the human mind that keep you from recognizing that you have Faith. It is God alone that makes the decision of faith and the act of faith possible. Faith never has come out of and never will come out of the belief of so-called understandings of the human mind.

Faith is that within you which decides to accept God's guidance, God's will for you. You do not actually live for God. You live and exist as the faith which lets God live in you. It's just a complete reversal of most religious teachings.

Faith is decision, the decision to act upon the reality of the grandeur and unity of the divine Self. The fallen man appears to have snatches of unity. He struggles to find a unity within himself that will give him a purpose for living, a purpose for existing. He seeks first one way to find a purpose in life, and then may make an about-face and seek an entirely opposite way; but he is always acting upon belief which he feels that he has obtained from the human mind and human reason.

Only through the decision which is God-given faith can man's fullness be integrated. In short, the act of faith is the unity of the fullness of man which appears sometimes to have been scattered all over the World of your own being.

It is not good human acts which save anyone for an eternal life hereafter. Good human acts, unless they be the by-product of the act of faith, are not really spiritually helpful. Haven't you seen people rushing around smartly and anything that comes along they will say: "What will we do about it? What will they think about it?" These individuals will always have an outside experience and they will always want to do the good human act, but it is finding another Realm.

Faith is the work of God acting through you and as You. Faith is God working in each individual who has but eyes to see Divinity at work. You don't have to make yourself believe and call that belief faith. It is only the coverings of human reasoning that keep you from recognizing what you are and who you are. You are Faith. You are Faith-in-action and that Faith is your birthright now.

You may find it helpful to ponder part of the second chapter of James in the Bible. There are many hints of what I have said and you will find some very interesting thoughts about faith there. For instance, that wonderful quotation: "Shew me thy faith without thy works." That is, can you show me thy faith by words alone, or by the statement "I have faith" or "I am faithful?" Faithful to something or to someone? But "Shew me thy faith," what you think of faith in the human realm, without decision and action, without thy works, "and I will shew thee my faith by my works," by my spiritual decision put into spiritual and human action.

32

Faith is both God-inspired and God-directed. Faith is the decision to act out of one's awareness of his spiritual Identity. And Faith becomes the essential act which enables one to enter the genuine universe of Spirit.

You are to show your faith by your works. It is the action of faith; and by the action of faith I mean the living of the Other World of reality — the saving Power which enables us to save others, to help others, to be God-in-action.

How does one gain this Other World, this world of spiritual Reality? By Faith and by Faith alone. Faith which is spiritually heard is discerned and acted upon. You are the Other World of Faith through which God acts. God acts through your faith, through your being Him in action.

Correctly viewed, you are the Faith of decision and action. You are made whole and live as the Other World of Faith.

VI

WIPING YOUR GOD–BLACKBOARD CLEAN

The very basic concept of God must be that God is ever-present. An absent God would be no God all. Ever-present implies the great truth that that which is ever-present—in this case God—cannot be absent. Yet traditional Christianity rests upon the erroneous concept that God and man are separate.

It is thought that while man resides in the material realm, God is somewhere else—in a heaven quite far from man, his confusion and even his human happiness. The great truth is that God is not separate from that which He creates, because He is ever creating man as His own Self.

The Law is that God, infinite spirit, is never absent from what He is eternally creating. Creation did not occur merely in the distant past. Creation is that which is ever going on as the outward expression in man of the ever-presence of God Himself.

34

God and man are eternally one. In thinking about himself, Christ Jesus expressed it as "I and my Father are one"—one Reality, one existence; yes, and even one Being—if the word Being is correctly understood. The only valid God is the God which ever remains at-one with that which He creates. Too long has man tried to prove—or unfortunately sometimes to disprove—the existence of God.

Equally so, this probing into God's reality or lack of reality has usually rested upon the premise of a God "out there" somewhere. In fact, sometimes the athiest glimpses something of Truth when he says that there can't be a God "out there." Unfortunately he has nothing with which to replace his statement; he has not found the sense of a "God within."

God—that is, the true and only valid God —is not "out there" somewhere. He is even closer than your breathing. He is at-one with you, the genuinely spiritual You, and you are and ever will remain at-one with Him. God's existence expresses Itself as You—expressing Him. His light is lived as You—expressing Him. God's love is proved through your living in accord with His love.

God's reality is your spiritual Reality. God is spirit. It follows then that—stripped of the ignorance you may have believed regarding yourself—you are also Spirit. Those who try to prove or disprove the existence of God miss that vital point—they try to prove God to be a "thing." The truth that God is spirit is the only valid and necessary evidence as to the reality and existence of the creative Spirit.

God and spiritual Man, your true Identity, are one, but you must be very careful that you do not think that you are the object of God's love, the object of God's life, the object of His existence. You are the spiritual You, the only valid You as God-in-action.

Have you ever thought that the truth or the falsity of God's existence is unimportant? What is important is that you live as God-in-action. The truth that you exist as a living, vital being is the only proof needed as to the existence of the creative Spirit.

You may say: "Can't I go to God if I have pain?" Your God is not a God that has the ability to stop pain or to give you pain. So often a traditional Christian will say: "If God has the ability to stop pain why doesn't he do it?" That individual accepts the premise that there is a God "out there," that in some mysterious way He comes to the individual and manipulates his human experience, turning a pain-filled body into a body free from pain. Or sometimes an individual will believe that God takes a good body and turns it into a pain-filled body. God doesn't operate that way. God is operating through individuals who are themselves, spiritual individuals or identities being God-in-action. Your God is the great Power within the spiritual You which alleviates pain.

If you are not alert you will turn with blind faith to a God that you believe is somewhere other than where you are and who is going to change a human condition. The human condition is only going to be changed by you expressing God. Or perhaps, hopefully, by someone else who is going to be expressing God, being God-in-action—as I've seen so often with a doctor or a nurse who comes and relieves the patient from the pain. What is the doctor doing? One may think that all he is doing is changing a painful body into a body that has no pain, but what is taking place is that the doctor at that moment is expressing the God-power.

You can walk through life like that doctor—as God-in-action. Or, unfortunately, you can seem to walk through life as one who wants his own way; who wants to turn a discordant condition into a happy condition; or maybe sometimes even wants to turn a happy condition into a discordant condition. The choice is yours.

"Choose you this day whom ye will serve." Will you serve your true Identity, or the misconception you have of yourself? Which are you going to serve? You're not going to serve God as the object which expresses His love to others. You must do it as God being Himself through and as you. You are not God's object helping to relieve the pain of the human body or the difficulties of worldly existence. You—that is the spiritual You—are God Himself in action, in action for instance in relieving pain.

We must realize that we have something special as part of Truth Center, a Universal Fellowship. We have something special to say to the world and it is not going to be something that we will say by "yacking," this constant talking about truth. It's going to be a living of Truth. When I say living Truth I mean living God—you as God.

Often we will want to be heard, yet we will only be heard when we are still enough and living enough of our true Identity as God-in-action. It isn't good enough to have a talking concept of God being present with you, it has to be a living force that you apply every moment of every day.

Traditional Christians usually have some concept of what they believe God is or what He is not. Usually these thoughts are of an absent God. But if you are going to gain the great Truth that I am saying, you need to basically give up your concept of an absent God. Someone will say that what I am talking about is a God not being absent or a God being present with us—as a talking concept. It's not a talking concept, it's a living concept so that those around you feel your life lived.

You must wipe the blackboard clean of your concept of a God "out there" somewhere. You must wipe the blackboard clean before you can really understand what I am saying. Then God will be able to write upon your heart, upon your mind. Unless you are willing to wipe that blackboard clean you will never really be able to come to grips with the great

Truth that God is ever-present and one with each individual now and forever.

Jesus put it so well when he referred to the seed which must die. "Except a corn of wheat fall into the ground and die." What was the seed? The seed was that which was believed to be truth. We think traditional religion is truth, yet we must let it die. We must let every concept we have of God and even every concept of a personal savior die before we can have the saving grace of God.

What is your God? I am hesitant sometimes about saying He is universal love, because the concept of love is so often misunderstood. We think of a mother loving a child — a mother separate from a child as merely loving a child; whereas, the love I am referring to is the love that you are.

God is perfect Reality. His existence is unique; it is unlike anything which is usually worshipped. You can worship Him only as you live perfect Reality. That's the only worship that is worthy of giving to God. You can worship Him only as you live perfect reality free from all limited and limiting views that you may have had of Him previously. You and your Father are one. You are ever at-one with and eternally existing as the ever-present God-in-action. My hope is that you see this great Truth that you are one with God.

Perhaps we have come to believe the concept that we are at the present time human but sometime we are going to gain spiritual

Reality, a spiritual view of ourselves that we are two selves. In the human experience it does appear that we are two selves—the material which is sensual, happy or unhappy; sometimes healthy, sometimes unhealthy; sometimes at peace, other times at war with ourself and with others. We believe that this is all there is to us—the one, a contradiction who believes he has sufficient funds to do the things he needs to do or insufficient funds to do the things he needs to do; the one who feels he is healthy one moment or with disease at another moment. This is the one who partakes of the tree of knowledge of good and evil. But this is not the man who is going to understand or be at-one with God.

The spiritual Man is the one who is free from contradictions. He is the You who exists as you drop all the coverings of your false education. When you drop all these coverings, then you become aware of this fact—no, you do not become aware of this fact—you are the living of God within your Self.

This You is the You of you and your Father—that which is the creative Spirit and You being one. You are at-one with and living as the ever-present I AM THAT I AM, bringing to mankind the realization that God is within each individual and never absent from him.

Truth Center, a Universal Fellowship, is dedicated in bringing to mankind the joyous news of this spiritual You.

VII

SUBMITTING TO TRIBULATION

There is one teaching that is common to all inspired teaching and that teaching is that spiritual Love must inspire—and result in—conflict.

If you have read the Bhagavad-Gita you may have been inspired or even disturbed, because the leading character is in what appears to be almost constant conflict —with himself and with others. And the Bible is filled with stories of conflict. When Christ Jesus came upon the scene he said: "I came not to send peace, but a sword"—conflict.

Inspired Religion enables one to meet conflict. It calls forth conflict and also enables one to handle conflict. But let me make it clear that there's a specific type of conflict that Inspired Religion calls forth. It is righteous conflict which you yourself must call forth. Inspired Religion must become to you a sword that you are to use. When you have these conflicts they become, not something that is a negative force in your life, but a very definite spiritual Force.

Whether we like to accept it or not, as long as we think of ourselves as a human, we are living in a universe where there is conflict. There is peace with violence, anger with patience, sickness with health and so on. These are the conflicts that come up, for instance, when we try to break with our past. We fail to realize that we have a new life, a new family, a new living, new experiences. People often find it very difficult when they read about Jesus in the Gospels where he is demanding that individuals leave behind their family ties. What he was asking them to leave behind was the misconception of family—and this brings a conflict.

Jesus was not in one sense a passive man, he was a man of action; or, more accurately, he was both a passive man and a man of action. When he saw that the money-changers were making the temple into a place of noise, of money lending and money borrowing, he took action. The unfortunate thing is that most individuals, particularly those who have come through a religion that teaches "peace, peace; when there is no peace," find it very difficult to spring into action. They want to sit on their hands. It's fatal for an inspired Teacher to say to such an individual: "You've got to do something," because they will say: "Don't say that to me. Leave me alone. Let me stay without action." But we need action.

We must have the conflict that flowers forth in a renewed spiritual Light. If there is no conflict we become figuratively the "fig tree" that stands there and is unproductive. We must have conflict, because the unproductive fig tree will never bloom. It has to be put aside for the spiritual Reality of one's own existence and that will invariably call forth action—conflict. You live as righteous conflict-in-action. You are called forth—and all Inspired Religion calls forth the greatness in you.

Traditional religion so often says that in order to follow a particular religion you will have a sense of peace or have a kingdom in the hereafter. What is needed is a living of the conflict right now—and the living of the conflict is the kingdom. The kingdom is not the realm of peace, because otherwise, in teaching about the realm of the kingdom, Jesus would not have said: "I came not to send peace, but a sword." The kingdom is not the kingdom of peace. It is the kingdom of righteous conflict.

You can judge if a religion is inspired or not by whether it demands conflict of its followers. If the religion tries to give "peace, peace; when there is no peace" it is not an inspired religion no matter how inspired it claims to be. Any religion that places its emphasis on qualities such as peace, harmony, abundance or health is an uninspired religion. If religion says you don't have to have conflicts in this life it is an uninspired religion. All Inspired Religions call forth conflict and we must expect conflict and expect it in our Now experience, right now.

The conflict that is merely an argument between two people, a war between two nations, isn't the conflict I mean. It is the righteous conflict within one's Self which Inspired Religion must call forth. It must call forth righteous anger. It must call forth, sometimes even toward a child, the anger of a parent who sees the importance that a child express obedience. The parent gets angry about it and that anger is better than leaving the child in his realm of disobedience.

Some people put up with conflict and they go around as a martyr for the rest of their lives, talking about the conflict that they had years and years ago. It is the facing up to conflict that enables one to gain spiritual Power so that he is no longer subservient to the conflict. Destructive conflict accomplishes nothing; or if it accomplishes anything, it's a negative thing that has destructive results. In fact, the one who engages in that kind of conflict often ends up by saying: "Oh, I had such a difficult time. I spent so many hours struggling with myself." All that one ends up with in that type of conflict is a self-righteous martyrdom. He sees himself as an individual who has gone through much suffering.

It is the Spirit that leads us to this purification problem. Spirit leads to conflicts. Everything that is accomplished is done so with conflicts. Have you ever known a child who formerly believed that two and two was five, and a teacher tries to say that two and two is four. The child has a conflict within himself because he's so convinced that two and two is five. He has to suffer that conflict and go through it until he is willing to accept the mathematical fact that two and two is four.

All conflicts   start with a conflict with one's self. It is the conflict, the suffering, the sacrifice of one's self expressed to others. It's not a selfish thing such as "I'm going to have this conflict with   myself." It will have the outward effect of blessing others and it always begins as spiritual Love.

What Jesus did   over and over in his experience was that in loving his disciples he sometimes demanded great things of them—and that love caused conflicts. This is true and at the same time untrue, because it isn't the love that causes the conflict, but the resistance to the demands that an inspired Teacher like Christ Jesus places upon his students.   What Jesus demanded of his disciples was that they seek the spiritual Realm rather than walking back and forth along the line of human development.   What caused the conflict was the disciples' resistance to that demand to enter the Realm "not of this world."

Inspired Religion must enable us to face up to and experience conflict—face up to and find the rewards of conflict. We don't need the Messiah that is so often pictured for us as a Messiah that brings peace; and we shouldn't be looking for a Messiah at some future time who will free us from conflict. But we need the Messiah of the cross, the one who was willing to go to the cross, to have conflict. It is only in the conflict of a cross experience that we are enabled to bless those on either side of us, or to bless our relatives, as Jesus on the cross blessed his mother. There is no blessing without the cross experience. The Messiah of the cross is that which is willing to give all, including conflict, that is, willing to engage in conflict for love. And this conflict must include those around us.

What do you do when somebody does something different, when there is the appearance of a conflict? You may have to have a big conflict within yourself, but do it you must. If you are facing up to the conflicts with yourself you will have conflicts with others in which some of the self-centeredness, self-righteousness, self-justification will be rubbed off. But it must be constructive conflict with others. Destructive conflict that merely argues back and forth humanly isn't going to take care of it at all.

What you see in another is what you see in yourself. Inspired Religion demands that we deal inwardly with ourselves and outwardly with others. In the Gospel of Thomas that's what Jesus was talking about when he said that the one becomes two and the two becomes the one. Unless we balance these two, the inwardness of ourselves and the outwardness with others, we either become self-centered or a mere human "do-gooder."

Jesus, when talking to his disciples, asked them: "Whom do men say that I am?" This statement is usually followed by trying to bring the disciples to a recognition of the Christly power. "But whom say ye that I am?" I sometimes wonder if Jesus didn't need that answer—if occasionally even the most inspired Teacher doesn't need to be told: "You are living the Christ; you are living the Power." If an inspired Teacher needs that reassuring, how much more do those with whom we come in contact need reassuring. Yet how often do we give that reassuring? When somebody makes a mistake do we criticize the mistake? Or, do we give them the reassurance based upon what we have seen of them in their divine Identity—that they are indeed the Christ in operation?

Have you ever thought that you are incomplete without this love conflict—without your peace and war, without your love and hate? This conflict—the war, the hate—is constructive conflict. Are you willing to engage in a conflict? It is the conflict that enables you to make your conflicts subservient to love; your wars subservient to peace; your hate subservient to love. And one has to get going and do it. Too long have individuals sat back and theorized about religion. Inspired Religion is that which crosses swords, a conflict within its followers.

It is not enough to endure conflict. Conflict must be used constructively. Then how will you know whether it's constructive conflict? It will be tempered with selfless, spiritual love. Constructive conflict is that which is inspired by the Spirit.

No conflict is an ending. Each conflict faced up to—and the benefit gained from it— leads to a new conflict. Do you suppose that Daniel in the lion's den, because he faced up to the conflict, never had a conflict again? The three Hebrew boys in the fiery furnace, did they never have another experience because they faced up to that conflict? But God is the God of conflict. After every conflict there is a renewal of life, a renewal of spirituality that enables you to face the next conflict with joy, with certainty, and certainly without this whining sense of "Please don't make me go through this, God."

The Spirit will not lead you into "peace, peace; when there is no peace." It will not lead you into the realm of: "Oh, leave me alone while I work this out—perhaps in a week." You won't work it out in a week. You must have the conflict at the moment the thing is presented ---"straightway." Only when temptation and acceptance of temptation come together is genuine spiritual growth assured. It's never going to come about by the avoidance of temptation. It is Spirit that brings you to temptation, to conflict.

What was Jesus' wilderness experience? What was the force which led Jesus to the conflict which we call The Temptation? One rendition of the gospel says that the Spirit straightway led him into the wilderness to be tempted, to have a conflict. It was the wilderness of conflict, certainly; but it was also in that very wilderness experience, coupled with it, the opportunity to prove his oneness and his wholeness with divine Life.

48

"And straightway the Spirit," one translation says, "drove him forth into the wilderness." Are you willing to be driven forth into the wilderness? Are you willing to let the Spirit drive you into the wilderness of temptation and conflict? The Spirit is ever driving you. And you will find that much of your unhappiness, much of your inability to find spiritual development is your unwillingness to let the Spirit drive you into the wilderness of temptation and conflict.

One of the most subtle forms of delusion is the fact that we think we need to be accepted. Read the temptation of Jesus and you will see that the tempter is trying to make him want to be accepted by the organized religion of his time. Do we also feel the need to be accepted by our families, our friends or sometimes even by our foes?

"If thou be the Son of God," if you are as spiritual as you think you are, what about all these material things you don't have? The point is that you don't need all those material things. The material things should come as "a result of," not because you need them or that they are proof of spiritual development.

Temptation, righteous temptation, if accepted and used, will enable you to prove that all material power is subservient to divine Spirit, that love is indeed the master of hate. And peace is the master of war, but we have to go on to the battlefield. Be an Arjuna, the character in the Bhagavad-Gita, that goes into battle. He didn't want to battle; but the story

49

says that he had to battle. We have to battle
with ourselves first; and sometimes, because of
our great love for and appreciation of another,
battle with others.

We don't try to avoid battle, we go into
battle. One traditional Christian hymn that I
both like and dislike at the same time is
"Onward Christian Soldiers." Usually it's
thought of as the Christian religion being su-
perior to every other religion. But the thought
I do admire is that we have to go forward into
battle with our banners unfurled. Are you willing to go forth into battle? Are you willing to
battle with the temptations that come to you?
Are you willing to go into conflict? Or are you
slipping back and being grateful for all the
material goodies you have? "We have a good
house, a good apartment, a good family," or
whatever it happens to be. Struggle with one's
self is the only real joy. The wonderful thing
about conflict is the fact that in this conflict
is the Light of your own being.

Have you ever thought that we need a
new view of God? God is that which is
constant change and unless we are constantly
changing, unless we are spiritually finding more
and more of our Self, we are not taking part
in His unfoldment for us. We need a new view
of God that is ever changing, not a God that
has a fixed principle that you can go to in an
almost mathematical way to find Him. So many
individuals want spiritual Truth to be "proven"
to them. You can't prove Truth, because
there's only one way that spiritual growth can
be measured; and it is by a life that lives in

the realm of conflict, through one conflict to another conflict.

If I were to tell you one thing it would be to go forward. Go to your Jerusalem—and your Jerusalem is your conflict that comes when you know that God is in you and will ever be with you to face the conflict. But you must go forward. You must leave behind all dependence upon anyone, yet at the same time, include everyone. You must find everything and everyone within your Self.

In closing, here is a quotation from my book "Dance With God" that fits very well the thought we have been talking about.

"Avoidance of tribulation is part of the worldly man's life. Submission to tribulation is part of the holy man's life."

51

VIII

THE BLOCK OF MARBLE

It is important to realize that the meaning of Truth, the definition of Truth, must be secondary to the living of Truth. Is our concept of the Truth merely a theory which we express in dogmas, in doctrines, in tenets or in teachings? Or is Truth something that is practical, that becomes a commitment, a concern? Which concept of Truth are you accepting?

Are you accepting the Truth that is a vital force for good? Or are you accepting Truth as a series of statements about Truth and calling that series of statements Truth Itself? Truth is not a set of statements, a series of things you call Truth. Truth is the living Force, the ever-changing, the ever-expanding, the ever-developing reality of Being Itself.

Frequently someone will say: "That is not what our Teacher means by Truth." What an inspired Teacher is presenting is not a series of so-called "truths." He is presenting a way of living. He is presenting Truth that by its very nature is the most practical thing that can be presented.

So often we want to fix our concept of Truth. We say Truth is "this" teaching. In mathematics it is a set of laws and rules such as two and two is four; and that is true as far as mathematics is concerned. But genuine Truth, spiritual Truth, found in the realm of divine Reality is not something that is fixed. We might even say that Truth is ever growing, ever developing, open-ended. Truth is a reality that is ever moving, ever changing. The movement is the reality of Truth; the change is the reality of Truth; the vitality is the reality—not an abstraction called truth. I have sometimes said that it would be better if we would think of God as a verb rather than a noun. The same can be said of Truth because Truth is a happening.

Truth is not a thing; it is not a saying; it is not even a teaching. And Truth is not a live teaching nor a dead teaching. Truth is not live facts nor dead facts, but Truth is that which is lived and which others can see through your life. Truth is not a teaching that you have heard and then shared as a lot of babbling words with others. Truth is a spiritual life lived and nothing else is Truth. Then how do we use Truth? We use Truth by becoming the living witness in relationship to others.

To use a comparison, Truth is the block of marble waiting to be made into a beautiful statue, but someone has to make that beautiful statue. Truth is ever waiting to be used, as that marble. It's ever waiting to be shaped, but you must shape it. All your talk about that marble is not going to make the beautiful statue. You yourself must do something. You must be the living Force through which—and as which—Truth operates.

Truth is also like the fruit tree. It gives forth fruit, but the fruit has to be taken off the tree, it has to be shared. It's cooked, it's prepared, then it's given to somebody or given to a family perhaps for nourishment. Truth must be that which, because it is used, provides nourishment. If it is not nourishing others then you can be sure that you have not found Truth. If you are not nourishing others—not through mere humanly good deeds, but through having found Truth Itself and its constant change— then you are not expressing Truth.

Jesus' command was to "know the truth." And how do you "know the truth?" You know it only when you can share it. You don't know the truth if it's an abstract truth to you. "Ye shall know the truth, and the truth shall make you free." Notice what Jesus said just before that. "If ye continue in my word, then are ye my disciples." Speaking to his disciples on another occasion he said: "Ye are my disciples if ye have love one to another." He didn't say you should gain the truth—a lot of abstract things you call truth—about what I have said, but that the disciples were to do something.

Living the truth, that is, loving one another, is the only way to be a genuine disciple and to "know the truth."

Truth is communal sharing; it is communal loving; it is communal living. Truth is never attained in the lonely belief that you may have regarding God and your relationship to Him. Truth is a living force and it is a living force in relationship to others. It is only through communal service that God-inspired, God-directed Truth is gained. It's not surprising that the early Christians saw this and they lived in communal service, concerned more with others than with themselves. They were not talking about just living together, but it was concern for others —by sharing, by living, by loving.

You must share the manna that you have digested today. You must have found spiritual nourishment and that spiritual nourishment must then be shared. You must share today's spiritual growth. It has to be today's manna that you have to share. Yesterday's manna, yesterday's gift from God to you is dead. This is a new day. This is the day in which you are to make practical the Truth you profess to have gained. You have no Truth unless that Truth is made practical through sharing.

Truth not shared is manna that has gone bad. Someone will say: "I've had a lot of truth given to me, but when it comes to sharing I can't do more than just a very limited amount."

The reason that an individual can't share is because he has let his manna go bad. He can't find any truth to share because all the truth that has been given to him has molded, become rancid.

It is a paradox that the easiest and at the same time the hardest thing to do is to spiritually and selflessly share with others. Viewed from the material realm you may be thinking about yourself when you say: "I just can't do that, it's impossible for me to do it." But viewed from the spiritual Realm it is the easiest thing to do.

You are to witness Truth yourself and as your Self. You are not to go teaching about Truth, teaching another person about Truth, teaching perhaps another nation about Truth, but you yourself are to live Truth. You are to be the witness of Truth. You are to do something about Truth beyond just talking about it. Truth isn't something to be learned, to be gained. The Truth you have gained must be lived—must be actively and selflessly lived.

You can never live Truth alone. Truth shared with others is the only Truth there really is; and through the experience of being with others, loving others, caring for others is found the only Truth that is genuine.

Truth is ever changing, is ever new. Only as you are willing to change, to become new every day, can you have Truth, this Truth which is ever available to you. Bury the truth of yesterday so you can have new Truth. Truth is alive. Live Truth. Be Truth.

IX

GOD BEYOND THE GULF

In order to teach we need words and words are helpful in presenting thoughts; but we have to remember that all words are subject to different interpretations.

For instance, if you take the word perfect in the statement "Be ye therefore perfect," what do we mean by the word perfect?

The word perfect or perfection has a variety of meanings depending upon the person who is using the word and also depending upon the person who hears the words. Some would say, free from sickness, in perfect health. Others might think of perfect as being in a perfect relationship such as "If I could just find a perfect husband or a perfect wife." I've even known people who felt that a perfect situation was when they were harassing somebody: "I put that person in his place. I had a perfectly wonderful time putting him in his place."

What about talking in theological terms when we give a name to God? Theology perhaps could give us the name that is given for thinking about God; but the question immediately arises—can we think about God? Can theology teach us to think about God? We have a multitude of definitions, theologian's definitions as to what God is and what his nature is. We try to define God, but we have to remember that the creative Force cannot be defined by words at all.

You might ask yourself: "What do I mean when I use the word God? What is the object or the character that I am thinking of when I use that word?" Eventually we are going to have to accept the fact that God is undefinable. The more we talk about God, very frequently, the less we have of God. We talk God out of our experience.

You cannot classify God, much as you would classify a person. You say such a person is an American; that one is a foreigner; that one is a musician; this one is a husband; that one is a wife. Yet we sometimes use words that would demand classification. We might say God is the father of all and because we make a classification, another group of people will come along and say: "No, God is mother of all." Or, "God is like a mother loving." Someone else will want to classify Him, not as father or mother, but as an "it." All of this is merely classification. Be very wary of a word which you use in an attempt to describe or classify God and His nature.

Perhaps you might say: "If I can't define Him and I can't classify Him maybe I can draw a comparison." Here again we run into a stone wall because God cannot be classified. God is that which is beyond comparison. Yet we keep saying: "God is like a river endlessly flowing;" or, "God is substantial like a rock." Now you have two different things. You have a river flowing and you have a rock. They are quite different. How are you going to classify Him? The moment you get into the realm of classification, at that moment, to some extent at least, you lose the reality and validity of the creative Source—lose it as far as your appreciation is concerned. But of course you can't actually lose it. We may use these classifications in teaching and in imparting, but certainly we must never believe that God is like anything. He's not like any person or any object. God cannot be classified like anything.

We now have definition, classification, comparison. Can't we use a name for God like we use when we talk about a friend? We talk about Fred or Susy; or sometimes we think of certain things such as a tree. But God is beyond a name. Moses must have glimpsed this, when instead of calling God, Jehovah, he recognized God to be I AM THAT I AM. While we must use a name in talking and teaching about God, the name is never God. We must watch that we never think of God as a thing or a person, because the moment you think of Him in this way you place Him in the class of things and persons.

We say God is the object of adoration, devotion or thoughts; but let me say very clearly that God is not an object that needs your adoration. God is not an object of anything. He is Himself creative Force. We have to watch that while we use adoration or devotion, that these are merely tools used, they are never the Reality. Then where does this lead us? We must come to the point where we recognize that God is One and is unique, not like something or someone else. He is not an object that you can turn to like you do to a Santa Claus and say "Give me goodies." God is not even a conception that you have in your thinking. He is inherently that which is imperceptible which the human mind cannot understand or can only distort.

We must stop seeking an undertanding of God, because God is beyond human comprehension. We must watch that we do not think we have to find something to compare God to, because God is beyond any comparison. Your concept of God, even when you say God is love or God is spirit, is not good enough. Of course we say God is spirit, but what do we mean?

If I am looking out the window and see those trees blowing in the wind, that wind is not seen. If we say God is that which is unseen, would we say the wind then is God because the wind is unseen? Even in using illustrations such as the wind being unseen, we have to be very careful that we do not think that by using these illustrations we are talking about God, because God is not seen.

The moment we use a word we immediately limit ourselves by what we understand that word to mean. Every time we name God we lose Him to some extent at least. I suppose names are helpful and it's helpful to know that that's a tree out there I'm looking at; that's a table I can see out there in the yard; that's a person that I am looking at now. But that is all they are — a means of identification in the human experience. Words cannot describe God.

Individuals will say: "We need a rational approach as far as God is concerned. We will rationally affirm God's reality and existence." That's not enough. You can't affirm something, you have to apply something. So we're going to have to find out what that something is. We're going to have to go beyond a mere rational approach to God, beyond even the arguments about God's existence. People will often spend hours saying: "Those poor athiests!" Then they will get into an argument with themselves or perhaps with the athiests about God's existence. You can't argue God into existence.

We have to go beyond any belief in God. We have to go beyond even a limited sense of faith in God, to God Himself. In order to do this one has to free himself from the limitations of philosophy and theology; because both of these dwell in the realm of the human mind. We must go beyond the gulf of limited human knowledge.

Does everything I have said up to this point leave you without a God, because you cannot define Him, cannot classify Him? Does this mean you have no God? No, your God is the God that is beyond the great gulf separating human intelligence, human knowledge, human wisdom from divine Reality. God is not something that is worshiped; He is that which is lived. You can only have your God as your life lived. Jesus referred to it as the Father in you.

Just think of yourself for a moment as if you were God-in-action. When somebody does something that you disapprove of, what do you do? What does the God in you do? Do you rush away and say: "I won't have anything to do with that!" Or do you become God-in-action right there? Do you live the divine Force there? You can't drag God to another location and find your peace.

So often we say: "If I could just get out of this discord," and we try to drag God into another area. It won't work; the discord has to be faced there and only there. God has to be lived right in the midst of discord. God lives. He is the living Force within you, but don't try to define Him and say: "He enables me to do good deeds to others."

The start of finding God is to look beyond the self-centered self, that which is always trying to protect itself and make itself acceptable. When you say: "I have to work this out, because it isn't right to let somebody get away with this," you haven't started with yourself. It is never with anyone else.

We don't have to worry about how anybody else is doing this. So often we try to get ourselves off the hook by saying: He or she, or the government or something else isn't doing it. This has nothing to do with it at all. Don't get off the hook; stay on the hook—don't run away. Prove it where you are, because God has to live in you, through you and as You right in the midst of what the human mind calls intellectuality or even the lack of intellectuality.

Sometimes I am very wary about saying: "God is love." It's a standard statement when you ask anybody what God is. They will say: "God is love." What do you mean by that? I've seen some things that are defined as love that it would be best to stay miles and miles away from. When Moses found God to be the I AM THAT I AM, he didn't say "I am the love that is love;" or, "I am the kind actions that are love." He merely left it: I AM THAT I AM. Even if you use that as a statement you are going to have difficulties.

We so often think God is love—that He's loving His creation. Yes, God is loving and He's loving His creation, but not in the sense that most people think of either love or creation. We say: "God is good," but what good? How do you define good?

My illustration is that of the lady who came to me and had had four husbands. To her, the good was getting rid of a husband and getting a new husband. That was her definition of good. Eventually she got rid of that husband and got another one; and in a short time she was back to see me telling me about how bad this husband was. It was exactly the same problem she had had with the previous husband.

We don't work the problem out by changing the situation, not even by getting up and leaving the situation. We stay in that situation and work it out. So when we say "God is good," what good are we talking about? Are we talking about moral good, divine good? That statement is only valid when the word good also becomes beyond definition.

If you can define what you think of as good you have not found God. Then what are we going to do? First you may start by just merely accepting the great Law that there is the divine Source that is omnipresent, omnipotent, omniscient. If you do that then you will stop making yourself the center of all presence, the center of all reality and existence.

You yourself must be the living God-in-action. God is not something or someone you actually worship—and I am referring of course in the ordinary sense of worship. But you do worship God when you are at-one with Him within your spiritual Reality.

When there is that Power within you, fathering His own nature in you, then you have found God; and He is lived as divine Reality within yourself. No one—not even the most inspired Teacher who has ever existed—can

65

give you an understanding of God on a silver platter. There is no understanding of God because God is a living reality.

Give up your search for an understanding of God and live God through selfless service to others.

X

WAR, AN ABSOLUTE NECESSITY?

Part of a sentence by Thomas a Kempis says that "All men desire peace." If all men desire peace then why don't we have peace? If desire is prayer then why isn't there peace? The reason that there isn't peace—even though all men desire peace—is that they fail to realize that peace comes only through warfare. The fact that there isn't peace is that mankind generally refuses to engage in warfare, that is, the right concept of warfare.

To desire peace and to refuse to fight for peace is to make half the system impractical. Yet the most practical way of finding peace is through a right sense of warfare. All men say they desire peace, failing to realize the absolute necessity for war in order to have peace. Christ Jesus taught this necessity of war and all holy Teachers teach the necessity of war.

That great Hindu masterpiece, the Bhagavad-Gita, would seem to be full of war;

and it deals largely with the necessity for war. The story of the Bible is also the story of one war after another, although sometimes the wrong concept of warfare. This is certainly true today because we're constantly hearing of "wars and rumours of wars." Just recently I was told that any time within the last decade or so there have been forty different wars— small ones, medium size ones, some very large wars—going on in the world at any one time.

Christ Jesus' words are still true. "Ye shall hear of wars and rumours of wars;" and then he said: "See that ye be not troubled." That is going to be the warfare—to find peace in the midst of "wars and rumours of wars." To be untroubled during warfare is the greatest war that you will ever have to engage in. Yet mankind gets all uptight when he has a war or an argument, perhaps with a neighbor. He fails to realize that he must engage in the inner warfare of being "untroubled."

Nation still rises up against nation. One political system rises up against another political system. One economic system or group rises up against another economic system or group. In the midst of "wars and rumours of wars" of whatever nature, we are to find inner peace through inner warfare so that we will be untroubled. Our great challenge is to be untroubled.

Jesus then makes a very amazing statement. He says: "All these things must come to pass, but the end is not yet." Do we accept the fact that there has to be an inner warfare expressed, often as outer warfare, because one is not engaging in the proper inner warfare? "But the end is not yet." The only end will be when you find genuine Peace within your Self.

Peace is never going to be found in the human realm. The peace which Jesus had must be found in the divine Realm or in spiritual Awareness. Peace must be found in an inner awareness of the necessity to rise up against all that keeps you from being your true Self, your true nature.

We don't have peace because we don't ask the creative Source of our being. We don't ask God for a solution. We ask a conference to straighten out the situation or we ask a summit meeting to straighten out the war in the world. We ask political and economic leaders to do it. Yet only the God within one's Self can give one peace. Only the active I AM THAT I AM has the power to give peace.

We spend so much time thinking about worldly peace and war. We will have conventions about peace, conferences about peace—all these things—and it will never work. The only practical way to peace such as Jesus lived is through inner peace found through inner warfare. Inner peace—this divinely inspired Peace—is the only practical solution to worldly peace or war. Worldly peace and war are not from God because God gives in the higher Realm. He gives genuine peace and genuine warfare.

es said it so well when he said: ence come wars and fightings among me they not hence, even of your lusts that .. r in your members? Ye lust, and have not: ye kill, and desire to have, and cannot obtain: ye fight and war, yet ye have not, because ye ask not." You ask in the wrong place, and that's asking not. You ask for peace where it cannot be found; you ask for it as if peace were merely a cessation of warfare.

J. B. Phillips in his translation of the New Testament makes that passage much clearer when he writes: "But what about the feuds and struggles that exist among you— where do you suppose they come from? Can't you see that they arise from conflicting passions within yourselves? You crave for something and don't get it; you are murderously jealous of what others have and which you can't possess yourselves; you struggle and fight with one another. You don't get what you want because you don't ask God for it." You don't go back to Source. Somebody else succeeds and you find it much easier to criticize that person's success than to look within yourself. The whole thing comes back to an inner warfare where you fight within yourself; and I'll tell you a little secret —if you fight within yourself sufficiently you won't have time to fight with others.

How do we start the struggle within ourselves? We start with things in daily life. Do we rise up against somebody rather than facing something within ourselves? Do we see the thing that they are doing wrong rather than struggling and suffering within ourselves? When someone doesn't do things the way you think they should do them, do you criticize that individual or stand in judgment?

"Ye ask, [for peace] and receive not, because ye ask amiss." You ask in the human realm. You ask for a war to end; and so often individuals will say to me: "Shouldn't we pray for the end of war in such and such a place?" If you could stop the war there it would only spring up in some other place. The only ending of war is through engaging in a warfare within one's self; and through that warfare, find this inner peace, which is also a continuous inner war to be what one is.

In the Psalms it says: "He maketh wars to cease," but only God can do it. "He maketh wars to cease unto the end of the earth; he breaketh the bow, and cutteth the spear in sunder; he burneth the chariot in the fire." Weapons of war will always disappear as individuals engage in an inner warfare; and this inner warfare has to start with you and with me.

What is this inner warfare? It's getting rid of all the accumulated habits that we think is our personality, the mythology that we have of ourselves. In the human realm we will have peace and war, but if we go to the God-power within, we have a warfare with ourselves that is at the same time peace. I'm going to give you a paradox, because all this seems a contradiction. In the spiritual Realm, warfare is peace and peace is warfare; and you can't have the one without the other.

71

Watch that you don't leave God out of part of His unfoldment. God is not only the God of peace, but He is also the God of war. He creates in you the ability to engage in the peaceful warfare of "self-analysis" and I am using analysis in quotes because I do not mean it as it is sometimes used. I mean the willingness to look at one's self and be what one is intended to be.

Here are some other remarks by Thomas a Kempis:

"No man may live here without some trouble. Therefore, he that can best suffer shall have most peace." This flies in the face of much of the religious teaching of the day which says that you declare peace. But that is the "peace, peace; when there is no peace."

It is the one who best suffers who has the most peace, the one who has the best warfare with himself that engages in the highest sense of peace. The one who sits back and tries to make everything as comfortable as he can for himself in the worldly experience can never have inner peace. Paraphrasing Jesus' words, how hardly shall the rich man who has everything enter the kingdom.

You must have—and be willing to engage in—the struggle with yourself, to suffer within yourself. "He that can best suffer shall have the most peace." He who avoids warfare may have what he calls peace, but this so-called peace eventually erupts in warfare again. Correctly used, genuine peace is suffering—that suffering of warfare within one's self. When I say suffering, I am using it in a specific way. By suffering I mean that struggle to give up the self-centered self so one may live at peace, the peace that "passeth all understanding"—all understanding about peace.

Here is the rest of that sentence by Thomas a Kempis:

"All men desire peace, but few desire the things that make for peace." How true that is! Very few desire the things that make for peace, because the things that make for peace are spiritual things. Few are willing to engage in self-surrender. Few are willing to give up the self-centered self.

The Old Testament is largely the story of the old type of peace, struggling to find peace by the subjugation of other people. So the Psalmist could say: "Scatter thou the people that delight in war." But the Psalmist thought of the people "out there." I wonder if he would have been willing to have said: "Scatter thou the people that delight in peace." Yet the one thought is just as destructive to one's spiritual progress as the other. One who feels he has a nice sense of worldly peace or personal peace is not going to struggle to find his true Self.

This struggle to find peace in the human realm just doesn't work. We've seen great pacifists and a so-called sense of pacifism has resulted either in a warfare with others or a destruction of the pacifist. The warfare is not

73

"out there." You have no one "out there" to make warfare with when you have this inner warfare. The whole warfare, this spiritual pacifism, is with your Self. This is the only genuine pacifism.

You are engaging in a continuous struggle, a continuous warfare, to find that inner peace which is your Self. But there is one great difference between this warfare and what we usually think of as warfare. This warfare never harms another. In that sense it is the only true pacifism. It is only a warfare within and with one's self, in which you leave behind your self-centered self. Such spiritual warfare is actually spiritual peace, because one is at peace only when he is willing to engage in this inner warfare. Then spiritual peace is spiritual warfare.

A statement of the Psalmist which almost sounds like self-righteousness says: "I am for peace: but when I speak, they are for war." It's the Old Testament teaching—the pre-Jesus time. It's always seeing "myself" as right, "they" are wrong. If you can engage in that kind of thinking you don't have to engage in a struggle, in a warfare, to be who God has created you to be. The Old Testament is the continuous story of the struggle to find worldly peace—of war versus peace and peace versus war.

What then is peace, the peace that Jesus said is not as the world views peace? First of all, we have to realize that genuine peace is more than the ending of warfare. Genuine peace is found free from worldly peace or even war. Genuine peace, the awareness of the inward teachings of Christ Jesus and other spiritual Teachers is the peace within, regardless of whether nations are warring against nations or whether nations have found a sense of peace.

When Jesus came he taught what all inspired Teachers teach, that peace is within. He said that "the kingdom of God is within you." Inner peace is the peace given by God. When one is at peace with himself, it follows as a necessity that he must be at peace with others regardless of how others act. The kingdom of peace is within you, but this peace is not as the world giveth peace. The peace that the world giveth can be changed at any time into war. The world will merely give periods of peace followed by periods of war. An inspired Teacher gives spiritual peace and this spiritual peace is a gift to you.

Peace is not impersonal or something that you can talk about as an abstraction. Peace is living at-one with your God-created Self and being that Self in action. Peace is the active doing, the being, the living, the expressing of being the fullness of God-in-action. It is what Jesus referred to as the Father in you. Peace is the living of the God in you. It is the asking of your God, the Power within you, to be peace-in-action.

Jesus said: "My peace I give unto you." He could also have said: "My concept of warfare I give unto you, but not as the world giveth, give I unto you."

Peace is not a thing attained. Peace is living in accordance with divine Law. Then spiritual peace and also, if I can use the word "spiritual-war", are you—living the God-power as You-in-action.

XI

YOU ARE
SPIRITUAL NOTHINGNESS

Most individuals go through their whole life seeking ego satisfaction. They try to find satisfaction in things, in other people, in other places. Yet it is in ego satisfaction that all the ills of the world are to be found.

Much of human existence becomes ego dissatisfaction—dissatisfied with where one is and with the situation under which one happens to live. All the time the suggestion is that individuals would find a greater sense of ego satisfaction if they could but acquire something outside of themselves. Individuals want someone to tell them how good they are, how brilliant they are, how helpful they are to other people or how young they are. In fact, all the problems of human existence start with the struggle for ego satisfaction.

You will never find your divine Selfhood so long as you are attempting to satisfy yourself in the search for ego satisfaction—in trying to satisfy the lower ego. You will never find your divine Self by building up your own self-centered self.

Some religions have built themselves around the thought that religion is to give one a greater sense of ego satisfaction. The ego is to be built up by the acquisition of things; and the acquisition of these things—they may be health, more abundance, a sense of perfection— is what religion is seemingly all about. It is not.

Then should you not have ego satisfaction in the human realm or replace it with a sense of lack of ego? I'm not saying that at all. Nor do I mean replacing things with a lack of things. That would merely be moving from things to lack of things. Just let things die in their importance to you.

You are not going to overcome this struggle for ego satisfaction by effacing yourself. You are going to have to do something much more. You must find a new, spiritual view of yourself. You must find the Self of nothingness, the Self that is completely happy —call it your own individual kingdom of heaven, call it Nirvana, or whatever you want to call it. But you must find the kingdom which Jesus said is "not of this world."

There is no genuine satisfaction in a self which is believed to be real and which often becomes a burden to you. Have you ever thought how much of a burden you are carrying by having to carry a sense of ego that you have constantly tried to satisfy? Self-satisfaction through human ego is a covering that you have put on around you and which you must eventually give up — either in this experience or in a future experience. Watch that you don't think that this individual that is seeking human ego satisfaction is your divine nature—it is not. It is the covering, the misconception, the illusion—whatever word you want to use—that you have accepted about yourself.

Whenever you gain ego satisfaction you must gain it at the expense of someone else; but in the realm of spiritual Nothingness there is no other person, there is only spiritual Nothingness. In fact, Nothingness is the realm of taking "no thought" about the outward, for the realm of Nothingness has nothing outside of its own Nothingness, its own Nirvana.

You may gain satisfaction in winning an argument over someone else, but you have given up your own identity; and you appear to have taken away the identity of someone else in winning your battle. Ego satisfaction or the struggle for ego satisfaction is at the back of every single human discord.

You struggle to be better, to find satisfaction in being better; but often that better is in the realm of the human ego. Eventually you must find your complete identity in the Self of nothingness, in the realm of "take...no thought for the morrow," to use Jesus' words. You must enter the Realm of no thing, no thought.

Take no thought of anything which may give you egotistical private pleasure—or problems for that matter. Stop thinking and acting from the realm of your own egotistical importance; because your egotistical importance is your own egotistical ignorance. It is your ignorance in which you believe you are right or you are wrong. Bury your egotistical ego in the soil of nothingness. Unless the seed which Jesus referred to, falls into the ground of nothingness and dies, there cannot be great spiritual growth. The seed of your human, egotistical self must be dropped, must die. For only as this is allowed to take place can you become aware of your divine Ego.

When you have become aware of the nothingness of your being then you will have found your Self, a Self that no longer has to struggle for satisfaction, because it is Itself—satisfaction and at the same time dissatisfaction. How are you going to accomplish this? Certainly it is not going to be accomplished by trying to get rid of the things that you think are important to you in your human experience. Always refuse to seek or to gain human satisfaction. Refuse to be mesmerized by the subtle suggestion that because things have worked out the way you want them to, that you are satisfied with the solution. Stop seeking satisfaction from something when you say: "I'm satisfied with my growth today." Or, "I'm dissatisfied with my growth today."

What you are going to have to do is to let the belief of a self, separate from a divine

Cause, just be blown out. In fact, in Sanskrit the word Nirvana means "blown out." It is a flame that is "blown out." Are you willing to let your self-importance, your self-ego or perhaps your lack of importance be "blown out?" Are you willing to be the Self—not separated from the spirit of Nothingness—expressing Itself in you and as You? Actually you find your divine Self when you permit the Infinite to "blow out" the flame of ego satisfaction.

When I talk about Nothingness it is the kingdom that cannot be seen as part of this experience. Nothingness is the kingdom "not of this world." It is the kingdom of Nirvana, when the candle is blown out and there is no flame—nothing to enlighten us, to brighten our way but the divine reality within ourselves.

Actually, the great need is just to let the ego be absorbed—not satisfied with itself, but be absorbed into the Infinite. This is where all that is of value—including beauty, the only lasting beauty—must be seen as this loosening, this absorbing of the divine Ego so that the misconception of the ego may pass away. The existence of the Infinite as You is the only valid Ego that you have a right to express. That Ego is the Ego of nothingness.

The extinction of the self-centered, self-ish ego that is always trying to satisfy itself, thinking that it is going to gain something through its victory of finding itself is the only way to find and to live the divine Self. Then why do you walk through this experience?

81

Certainly you walk through it to do more than merely find satisfaction in the personal ego— or dissatisfaction for that matter. You are here to let the personal ego and the satisfaction or dissatisfaction it may bring, die in the soil of Nothingness so that you may find, live and be the divine You. This divine You is the Nothingness of divine living.

Some of you may be saying: "Give us some practical advice on how we can let this flame that we think of as ourselves be blown out." I could give you some practical advice and here are a few suggestions. I could give many more—but here are some things you can start with:

Be very careful that you do not become "involved" in the problems of human living. We spend so much time struggling to adjust the human situation into a way that we think is perfect, good or right or even beautiful. That does not mean that you should not be involved in human problems. But involvement must come as a result of your having found something of your divine Self.

See that you do not become emotionally attached to that which is going on around you. If you do become emotionally attached, you will sink into the problem and you will try to find satisfaction in the adjustment of the problem.

Be watchful that that which is of little or no importance in the great view of things does not become overly important to you.

82

Learn to look at your problems and also your victories objectively. Both the problems and the victories are not you. Refuse to identify yourself with them. Refuse to become involved with them mentally; and above all that you do not personalize them.

As indicated in the Gospel of Thomas—be a "passerby." Just learn to treat everything as an interesting experience, a new adventure which you may view. That little word view is a big help, because we look on the object, but we do not identify ourselves with it.

Another thing that may help you in a practical way is that when something annoys you that you don't become angry. Be a "passerby;" that is, change your view of the person who is causing you the problem and of the problem itself. Refuse to personalize the difficulty through which you are going or even to personalize the person.

Be the spiritual Nothingness, the Nothingness which no incident in the human experience can possibly touch. No matter what the situation may be which may come into your experience, you can rest securely in your being the spiritual Nothingness. Do not become a something which must defend himself or someone else. Be the passerby. You are not a thing or person that has to rise to every situation which presents itself. You are the Nothingness which can pass by the thing that is claiming to be the somethingness. Does this mean that this awareness of your true Identity has no effect in the human experience? To

83

those looking on there may appear to be an adjustment or a change in the situation.

It was because Jesus expected his students to rise as he had done by being "lifted up," that he could draw unto him all that needed healing, all those that needed care. But all of this was to be an external experience. All the adjustments that take place in the human experience must appear, at best, as but a by-product of living your spiritual Nothingness.

All the problems that you have ever faced or will ever face have at their core the mistaken belief that you are an independent ego, and as an independent ego you are always gaining or losing something. Ego is but a thing that you have thought yourself to be. You are not an independent ego; you are not a thing. You are spiritual Nothingness and you must eventually realize that all there is to your identity is your Nothingness. Jesus' statement: "And I, if I be lifted up" will enable you to enter the Realm where you are not influenced, hampered or exhilerated by the somethingness of a human ego.

You are on the journey to the finding of the Self of nothingness. To find the selfless Self is to find nothingness, to want nothingness, to need nothingness. But I must caution you that I am using the word nothingness in a very unique and perhaps special way. I'm not using nothingness as merely the absence of something. Nothingness is the freedom to live, freedom to be unencumbered by things or situations.

You already have your Self of nothingness. It is your divine Self right at this moment. It is complete and it is whole. Your divine Self bespeaks the serenity which comes from the awareness that you are no longer the compulsive seeker of satisfaction in the self separate from the Infinite.

Spiritually viewed, you are spiritual Nothingness. You've come from spiritual Nothingness and you are on the path which will eventually return you to spiritual Nothingness.

You are the Self of nothingness.

XII

WRESTLING WITH
THE SPIRITUAL ANGEL

You are engaged in a journey, a journey that not only takes place in this experience, but in a previous experience and an experience that will come after this experience. Whether you accept it or not, you are engaged in a journey. What you do along the way of that journey determines the success of the experience through which you are going.

You are taking part in a journey and where is that journey leading you? It's leading you to the very center of your being, to the wholeness of your oneness with the All. You may be off on a detour; you may feel the journey is a rugged one; or you may just be sitting by the side of the road letting your head bask in the sun. But you are on the road to finding, being and living your wholeness, your oneness, your completeness with the All.

What is this journey? It's very much like going to school; and school wouldn't be very productive if occasionally the teacher didn't give you tests. Life is a series of tests to see what you are gaining out of the experience through which you are going, to see what you have learned. More important than to see what you have learned, the test is to see how you have applied yourself.

What these tests will be, you cannot know. When they will come and how they will come, you cannot know; but tests there will be. They will come to you like the "thief in the night." You will either be prepared or you will be unprepared. When these tests come you will do one of two things. You will either pull around you your past experiences and build a bigger covering so that you don't have to face up to the experiences, or you will accept the test, stand up to it and take one step forward towards your spiritual Oneness. The covering is merely that which gives you a temporary sense of security—but actually it's an insecurity.

Everything in life is a test; although some tests in life will stand out more vividly to you. The point is, what do you do with the tests that come to you? Do you use them as opportunities, as adventures, as wonderful challenges? Or do you say: "I don't see why these things have to come to me. I don't see why I have to pick up a cross. I don't see why I have to have a difficult experience." You can either accept the tests that come in life as adventures, as challenges, or you can go into a realm of despair and say: "Why me?"

It is the self-centered self that wants things done your way. This doesn't mean that you turn things around and want it done the way somebody else wants it done. You want to do it the way that infinite Spirit wants it done. It is using every test as an adventure, as an opportunity, to prove the unity that one has as his birthright with the Whole. If one is using every problem that comes to him that way he becomes the master of the event, master of the test.

What are you doing with your journey? Your journey must be the journey of the glory in the tests, the glory in the trials. You must see glory in every problem that comes to you. It is joy in tribulation. Those who have a spiritual Teacher to help them along the way are fortunate, for they can call upon his Power to help them. They can use that power, but they can use it only in the ratio that they themselves are striving to conquer the self-centered self.

We are not here to try to control outside events. Unfortunately that is what the Western religions and life seem to indicate. We use our prayers to try and adjust the human scene; we pray for help; we pray for peace. Am I saying you shouldn't pray for these things? I'm not saying that at all. What I am saying is that this is not the highest sense of prayer. The highest sense of prayer is the prayer that leads one to fight the good fight with one's self.

You are not to be masters because of an event. You are to be masters in spite of events around you that are taking place. You do not respond to the event because it is "out there" pushing itself upon you, but because you see it as "in here," as an opportunity to grow Spiritward. As you use your events this way you will find that there is great freedom for you in rising up to meet these challenges. As you do, you will find in varying degrees, the liberation to be your selfless Self, so that while these events go on outside of yourself they are no longer your master. You have your freedom to meet the test that they present without becoming part of the conflict.

Did you ever stop to ask what is a spiritual Teacher's greatest joy? Certainly one of them is when students endeavor to face up to the tests that are presented to them. Or more accurately, when a student uses the test to stand, "and having done all, to stand." Stand, rather than getting into the problem, trying to adjust, trying to manipulate, trying to fight against somebody or a group of people, but stand instead of giving way to the problem. In short, students need to learn to use the problem as a test.

One of the things you can do is to accept the demands placed upon you by a spiritual Teacher. But this acceptance cannot be grudgingly given; it must be given from the heart. It cannot be a "no" that you want to then turn into a "yes." "No, I can't do that; yes, I'll do it if you want me to."

When tests are presented, often there is great resistance even to what a spiritual

Teacher is trying to convey to a student. "Don't bother me! Don't say that to me!" Students often want the theories that the Teacher is presenting, but do not want to use or apply truth. And there grows up a resistance to this using, to this appplying, to this being the Truth that the spiritual Teacher is presenting.

There's no resistance to what the Teacher is presenting if the Truth is something that makes one feel just a little more comfortable in the human experience. There's no resistance if it is just a nice, comfortable theory about life. But a spiritual Teacher needs much more from his students. He needs the surrender by his students to their selfless Self. He needs life lived in response to the trials that are presented. I am not talking about fighting in the human realm against the trials. It is rising to the fullness of one's own being—and living from that point of view.

A spiritual Teacher doesn't need his students' praise or adulation. He needs students who will strive to meet the tests that life presents. Very frequently students will try to "get around" what the Teacher is demanding. They will substitute for living what the Teacher is saying by quoting the Teacher or by glorifying the Teacher. Yet the only valid gift a student can give to a spiritual Teacher is his self-surrender and nothing else is a genuine gift to the Teacher. What a spiritual Teacher has given to his students as the truths that he has presented can only be appreciated when they are actually lived. Every test that is presented to the student must be used as a steppingstone Godward.

You are not here merely to care for the body, to be overly concerned with its pains or its pleasures. You are here to prove that the body is not the limiting force that it seems to have been. I do not mean by this that the body will not respond to your spiritual growth, but this response is just a by-product. Take good care of the body, but leave it as much as possible out of your thinking.

Somebody will probably say: "I am meeting the test with prayer and meditation." Can you? Of course not. Supposing you wanted to keep the sun from rising tomorrow. You said: "I would like a nice quiet day so I can sleep all day. I'd like it nice and dark. I'm going to pray that the sun won't come up tomorrow." I defy you to pray and pray, meditate and meditate to keep that sun from coming up. That's not the purpose of meditation. Meditation of itself is never part of the journey. It is the respite in the journey.

Practice your meditation, respect your meditation, love your meditation, but don't expect meditation to do what it cannot do. I'm not saying you shouldn't engage in meditation and prayer, but meditation can go a long way to giving you a deeper sense of peace, and perhaps even a right sense of rest, which will prepare you for your journey. But you must take the journey.

Meditation cannot take you one step along your pathway to the finding of your divine Selfhood. It may be the quietness and the certainty that you need to generate health so that you may get ready for the journey, but the journey is a series of mighty wrestlings with yourself. It is the facing up to the tests, some of which you may appear to win—others you may at times even appear to lose. But the warfare with this self-centered self that wants its own way is all-important to your spiritual development. Nothing can take its place. There is only one way that you can meet the test and it is by spiritually applying, living, being. There's only one way you can do it and that is by refusing to justify, or for that matter condemn, what the human eye has seen.

What do tests do for you? They provide you with the opportunity to surrender to the greater Self, the selfless Self, the Self that asks nothing for itself. The Self is nothing being nothing, expressing nothing, not needing anything. In a previous talk I mentioned the word "nothing" in a unique way, not using it in the usually accepted definition of the word.

You are not the only one who is given tests. Everyone is given tests. It's part of walking through this life, because life is a series of tests. The one who makes the most of his journey is the one who uses these tests as a means of taking a small or perhaps a great step forward. As you pass through your life of tests a spiritual Teacher may give you guidance, but even he cannot do the spiritual work for you. The spiritual work you must do yourself.

As you go through life your journey will depend upon following the guidance that has come to you in every test that is presented. You are not alone in the tests that you have to face up to. And knowing this makes you quite unique; because you are aware of the fact that in that test is God.

Let me read part of a Biblical story of an individual who was faced with a test of his unfolding spiritual development. You remember that Jacob had mistreated his brother. He had stolen from his brother what his brother had a right to have. Then he was to face his brother and he began to have great fear.

"And Jacob was left alone." That's where all reformation has to take place. It's so easy to say: "If so-and-so would do something different then I would be able to handle this problem, this test." It's willing to be left alone. Are you willing to be left alone? Because it is in one's aloneness that the wrestling takes place.

"And there wrestled a man with him until the breaking of the day." Remember, the "man" was an angel. So often when we see a little light, we get just a breaking of the day, and we say: "I've got the lesson" and off we go. At times, as we come up to a problem we see something, we see the break of day; and then something goes out of whack and we slip right back to where we were before. We have to wrestle more.

With every trial comes the angel. Every trial has its angel to wrestle with. We so often think of angels as angels of peace, but actually the more spiritual angels are the angels that wrestle with us.

"And when he saw that he prevailed not against him, he touched the hollow of his thigh; and the hollow of Jacob's thigh was out of joint, as he wrestled with him."

Most people try to get rid of tests. They say, "I must get rid of this sickness; I must get rid of this pain; I must get rid of my conflict"—without having faced up to and demanded the growth that enables the individual to see his own Peniel. But what did Jacob do when he first saw the break of light and saw that he was slipping back? Did he say: "I'll just give up, I'll go to sleep?"

"And he said, Let me go, for the day breaketh. And he said, I will not let thee go, except thou bless me."

Every problem must be met that way. "I will not let thee go except thou bless me." Are you willing to wrestle until the break of your day—and beyond? If you are willing to wrestle and then beyond, your nature is changed. Every test faced up to becomes a wrestling, a wrestling with an angel. But you must not let that angel messenger that has come to you through that test go until you have found the blessing that it has in it for you.

"He said unto him, What is thy name? And he said, Jacob. And he said, Thy name shall be called no more Jacob, but Israel."

You are no longer the one who is struggling to be self-satisfied, to justify yourself, to say: "Why doesn't he do something?" or "she do something?" Find your Israel within yourself.

"For as a prince hast thou power with God and with men, and hast prevailed.

"And Jacob asked him, and said, Tell me, I pray thee, thy name. And he said, Wherefore is it that thou dost ask after my name?" Because there is no name for it.

"And he blessed him there." He found his blessing.

"And Jacob called the name of the place Peniel: for I have seen God face to face, and my life is preserved."

Find this spiritual Life. Find the Life that is your life—face to face—with God.

When you are willing to take each test as a wonderful opportunity to prove that your self-centered self cannot stand in the way of your Being, your Reality, then you see God face to face as You—as your Self.

XIII

AN EXPLOSION

Mankind seeks fervently for some way to make things better—for himself, for his family, for his nation, for the world. In so doing he turns to many different avenues such as a religious teaching. He turns to political leaders and to political systems in an endeavor to make things better. More recently he has turned to psychology and philosophy.

To sit back and say we can make the land produce so much more crops or that we can now produce so many more atomic bombs is an indication that we have forgotten what progress is all about. We live to express progress, but the progress we are called upon to live is not the usual concept of progress. Then what is progress? Progress is the means or is the external realization and activity of a continual unfoldment of God within individuals.

It's true that political systems, philosophy, psychology and religious teachings may point the way, but sooner or later we must find progress in a different realm. We must find progress as an inner unfolding of God's own goodness within us—expressed to others.

All of which brings us to the question: can we pray ourselves to more progress? Can we meditate ourselves to more progress? Of course there are many different interpretations of the words prayer and meditation. Sometimes the words are used interchangeably; but to be specific, prayer is asking for something. Prayer is asking for peace, for prosperity, for health; whereas, meditation is—at least in theory—a means by which one finds peace with himself. He finds peace through meditation.

Meditation is not another solution in opposition to other human solutions for this desire for progress; nor is meditation a means of solving problems, although the by-product may well be that problems are solved. If you meditate to solve problems your meditation has to be in the human realm. The meditation that I am talking about is the meditation that is "not of this world."

We have to accept the fact that problems exist and that problems become more aggressive to us when we unite ourselves with the self-centered self. When we use meditation to gain something for ourselves we are placing ourselves on the line of human thinking. We merely move back and forth from a sense of confusion to a sense of human peace in which the human mind says that it is at peace.

You do not meditate to solve problems, but the by-product may well be that many problems disappear when you gain and live a new view of yourself. You cannot have the one without the other. If the new view is not lived you have not really found it.

Often what is called meditation becomes a negative force which merely becomes quietness in the human realm. We have a lot of courses now on "how to meditate, how to get still" when everything around us is in confusion. Genuine meditation is not that meditation. Genuine meditation is not making the human mind to be still. Genuine meditation is becoming aware of one's individual listening to Divinity. In short, you do not create the means to meditate, you become the "receptacle" into which God is putting His love.

The self-centered self cannot find nor take part in genuine meditation. You cannot affirm yourself into a state of meditation; you cannot pray yourself into meditation. You can only meditate when the self-centered self is cast aside. Jesus indicated this when he referred to the seed that falls into the ground and dies. Unless the seed falls! You have to let it fall. Don't hold on to this seed and try to look and see if it's growing. Let it die.

You cannot break your seed in two and let part of it die, saying: "Yes, I'll let this little bit of my self-centered self die." You need to give up the whole seed, let the whole of the seed fall. All self-centeredness must be allowed to die. This doesn't mean that you go through a harassing experience with yourself in which you set out to try and make the self-centered self die. You just let it die. Only as that is done will you be able to experience your already God-created, spiritual Self.

Be careful that you do not think that you can manipulate this self-centered self into meditation. Then what is meditation? What do you need to meditate? It is to let the self-centered self die. Only the selfless Self is capable of genuine meditation and finds its source in God Himself.

Meditation is that which enables you to become aware of what you mean by "I." You go through life talking about "I." "I am sick; I am well; I am prosperous; I am in poverty." I, I, I. Many of your problems will come about as you go forward in your adventure Spiritward because your concept of "I" has become fragmented. Part of the time you think of this "I" as gaining something for yourself because you want something, need something; at other times it will be: "I would like to be my God-created Self."

Meditation enables you to find the unity of that "I" within yourself. You do not try through human will to get rid of the "your self-centered self," but because you know your God-created Self, your self-centered self dies—not the other way around.

Meditation is not a means of accomplishing something. You do not meditate to accomplish anything. You cannot have a human reason for meditating, because meditation is not the accomplishment of something. Meditation is the accomplishment— if I can use the word accomplishment—of nothing, not even the ability to meditate. Meditation is merely letting God be you. That's all that genuine meditation is. It is when the blackboard is completely cleared so that God can write upon it.

The by-product of that letting of God be you may well be that it prompts you to selfless activity—and that prompting must be heeded. If you meditate and then don't take care of the sick, don't take care of the dying, then you have not really meditated. What meditaton prompts you to do, you must do; but it must be a by-product and not something real in itself. It must be that freely receiving, freely giving. A statement found in the Gospels says "heal the sick, raise the dead" and it gives four different things you are to do. Then it says: "Freely ye have received, freely give."

Meditation is the free receiving of God as You; and then meditation must be the freely giving of God as You to others. I often wonder if people who quote the first part of that statement ever read the rest of Jesus' command; because it is not only to take care of the human situation, it is to freely receive, freely give.

Frequently I have said that you have to be the selfless Self in order to meditate. This then brings up the question: What is the self-less Self which meditates? The selfless Self must be a "no thing." It cannot be something that is defined. If it could be defined it would be in the human realm. This selfless Self is not part of your being, it is your Being Itself. It's not like having a chair and we say we have a leg to the chair. It's not like the leg to the chair, it is the whole chair.

The selfless Being is your entire spiritual Reality and it can be "known" only as Reality. It can be only "known" as Being. It is God "knowing" you—not the other way around. All religion reverses this process, saying you are to know God — as if you were an independent agent that has some special ability to know God. Actually it's the other way around. Meditation is God "knowing" you. The reason for quotes is that God isn't knowing in the sense of a thought process.

Meditation is the "secret place;" and what is the secret of this secret place? It is the God who must forever remain a mystery. The selfless Self that is one with God must also remain a mystery. So often in talking to individuals, they will say: "Just explain it to me in a way that I can understand." That individual wants God explained in terms of human thinking, but it has to remain a mystery. The mystery has to remain a secret; it has to be found as something that is nothing, "no thing."

Your selfless Self is the secret which only the divine Source can reveal; and it reveals it in you and as You. This discovery of the self-less Self should be an inner explosion in which the other self is blown away by that very explosion, but leaving intact the spiritual, selfless, holy Self.

Meditation should not be a quiet thing as we usually think of meditation, but meditation should be that which explodes, which is vital, which is doing; and which you never have to tell anyone that you are meditating no matter how close that individual is to you.

Meditation is an explosion, an explosion which leaves nothing but the selfless Self—your original Self. It will not leave you with a new Self which you can picture with the human mind. The Self will be free from the need of that picture. The selfless Self is simply your spiritual Self. It is your Self beyond description. It is your Self beyond the acceptance of the limitation of the limited and limiting human mind. This spiritual Self is the Father in you. Jesus uses the expression "The Father in me," and what he said to his disciples applies to you. This spiritual Self is the Father in you expressing Himself as You in your relationship to everything in your experience. This spiritual Self is the Father living in you. This Father living in you is the only "thing" we can call spiritual perfection.

God and the spiritual Self are but one— the Father in you, or as Jesus said: "I and my Father are one." I often refer to the spiritual

102

Self as the divine Self; and the only way one would have difficulty with that expression is to think of God as something separate from their Self. But you and God—the spiritual You and God—are the divine "I." Become aware of this—realize it—and you will no longer live a fragmented life which will cause you so many problems. We spend so much time thinking that we are just a mortal who has to make progress and acquire things for himself, his family, his nation, or even the world; and then at other times he is the spiritual Self. Meditation enables you to free yourself from a fragmented sense of your "I."

God and this spiritual Self exist as One and are One; and God is not an object separate from this spiritual Self. The spiritual Self is not something separate from his God. God and the spiritual Self that is You have always been, are now—and ever will be One. There's no room for duality here as if we are here and God is off there some place. God is within you expressing Himself as You.

What about all this turmoil in the world around us? What about the world around us? The spiritual Self includes the world around you. We might even say that the spiritual Self includes the world which we have thought of as objects outside of ourselves. This spiritual view of the world is totally different from the way that the self-centered self sees the world. The selfish self starts to make its progress through the manipulation of people and objects. It interferes with the natural flow of nature by building dams. I'm not saying that dams are

103

wrong; I'm just saying that this is the way we think we can control nature.

"If that person would just think differently it would be so much easier for me, so I'm going to set out to manipulate him!" Or he will try to manipulate events: "If this event had happened in a different way, things would have been different." But the selfless Self has no need to manipulate things, no need to manipulate things for profit, happiness or health.

The selfless Self has no wanting for things, no greed for things, no mad struggle for things. Because this selfless Self has no need for things, it has no fear about the loss of things. As one becomes aware of his selfless Self he also becomes aware that the objects are actually himself; and these objects are not seen then as needed or not needed. Because they are needed or not needed there is no attraction to the dependence upon objects. In short, the selfless Self sees and experiences what Itself is and nothing else.

Up to this point you may have thought of other objects as "out there," things pushing in on you. As you become aware of your selfless Self you see that these objects are not limitations. When you see that the objects and everything that you see is your Self, these objects thus viewed, instead of competing with the selfless Self, become complimentary to and part of the selfless Self. The "I" which is your selfless Self is ever meeting the object which one has called another thing, another person.

The spiritual Self forever finds unity with the world of objects or what he has previously thought of as objects. The spiritual Self is forever finding unity with the world of others. This unity is what is essential if one is to live as the spiritual Self.

The spiritual Self is united with all—all that one has previously thought of as outside of himself, as objects "out there." The spiritual Self is united with all by Love and you cannot affirm or deny this Love. Love is not really something that is said, although Love may express Itself as something said. Love is lived —as the spiritual Self expressing Itself in relationship to another or others.

It is of paramount importance that one learn that all spiritual meditation has to express itself in group action. The selfless Self cannot be lived alone—cannot be lived by going into a monastery and shutting out the world. It cannot be lived in the quietness of a house or an apartment. It has to be lived as part of a group.

Jesus put it so well when he said: "Where two or three are gathered together...there am I in the midst of them." He didn't say "I'll come to you as individuals." The Self will be lived in the relationship of the two or three, the thirty, the three million or the three billion; but it will be lived in relationship to others.

105

One is alone with the allness of his oneness with his God. He is alone with all that God has created. The only one who can engage in this spiritual meditation is the selfless Self. The only one who can spiritually meditate is the one who actively lives with others as his eternal oneness with his God.

To meditate—that is, genuinely meditate-is to joyously and lovingly submit yourself to God's will for you. At the same time, to meditate is to be aware of the reality of God's will as it applies to others.

To meditate means letting this oneness with God express Itself in and as the activity of your daily life.

Genuine meditation is this awakening to your great, spiritual Self.

XIV

GOD NEEDS YOUR THANKS

Would you encompass the whole world in love today? Giving thanks is the way. Giving thanks is the means by which you encompass the whole reality of creation.

You have been created to be a joyous "thanks giver." You have been created to give thanks joyously. And why is it necessary for you to give thanks joyously? Because God is using you as a chosen vessel to give His love to the world. If you will but let Him, God also uses you to share His goodness and His love with others. You can be grateful to the divine Source, for what He gives, He gives through chosen vessels so that you and others can be a chosen vessel.

You can be a joyous thanks giver, because not only is God using you, but He will send His love to you through others. He will send His love to you through friends, and especially through enemies—the ones you may not get along with—they are God speaking. Rarely do we receive anything directly from God. We receive through someone, through a friend, sometimes through some thing and sometimes through a stranger or even an enemy. If we are not alert we will feel that God speaks to us directly—and indeed in some sense He does. More often He will speak with us indirectly through a friend or it may be through someone whom you can't understand because of the way that he or she acts.

How does God's goodness become evident to us? God is speaking to us all the time by everything that comes into our experience. Not only does He speak to us through what we think of as individual people, but He is speaking to us through everything in His universe. He gives us His abundance—in the fruit from a tree and the vegetables from the earth. He gives us His abundance through others and through things. God uses others and things in His creation to share His goodness with us. The divine Source sends His goodness to you so that you may share it with others. Be grateful that He sends His goodness to others so that that goodness can be shared with you. You can be grateful, not only that you have God to give to others, but that others, especially your enemies, have God to give to you.

You need to thank the Source for the good that you are receiving and that others are receiving. Intuitively, mankind has realized throughout the ages that God needed to be thanked. We had this giving of thanks in ancient times when people gave the first of the flock or the first-born lamb. The Source needs to be thanked. We need to give to the Source what the Source has first given to us. We give back to the Source and that giving back to the Source is what we call the giving of thanks.

You need to go through life returning to the Source what the divine Source has first given to you. And how do you return to the Source what the Source has first given to you? Through joyous thanks-giving. The Source is nourished by your thanks. So often someone will say: "God doesn't need anything from us, but we need from Him." God needs your love returned to Him. The Source, God, would be poor indeed without the thanks and the love of His subjects.

Why did the Source create you? So He could glory in the grandeur that is you. Why did He create the universe? So He could glory in the grandeur of His creation. The divine Destiny is completed through your willingness to return to Him through thanks the grandeur that He has first given to you. Be thankful, be grateful, be joyous for all the Source has given to you—the fragrance of new-mown hay, the song of the bird, the beauty of the flower, the comfort of companionship.

Give the Source His due. Thanks given to the Source is the great transaction needed between you and your Creator. Every time you express selflessness you are thanking God, for you are expressing Him, you are living your spiritual Self. The selflessness which you express is the greatest thanks that you can give. God needs your thanks.

One needs to cultivate the ability to thank God even when one might feel that there is no reason for thanking Him. Thank Him in sickness; thank Him in poverty; thank Him when there are "wars and rumours of wars." I do not mean that there is any particular virtue in being sick, in being poor, or being the victim of war. But these opportunities—and that's what they are if they are viewed correctly—provide us with the means by which we can look beyond the limited view of ourself. We can look beyond and see the greatness that we are, "the chosen vessel" of God, a way in which God shares His goodness.

You must be able and willing to see the Source shining in all its brilliance right in the midst of the problems of life. Give thanks, not because you have material abundance or because you lack material abundance, but because it is your duty to be thankful. You are not wealthy because of things you have, or poor because you lack certain things. You are wealthy if, despite what the outward is presenting, you express thanks.

Watch that you don't spend all your time expressing thanks for the external things that you have accumulated. You will never become aware of your natural greatness given to you by God by looking at the things you have acquired, even at the things you think God has given you, or by mulling over a group of what

110

you call "spiritual truths" which you think you have accumulated. If you are using your truths only in order to do things, you haven't found God, nor are you thankful to Him.

There is only one way that your greatness can express itself. It is by returning back to God through thanks the things He has given you. Ponder again Christ Jesus' story of the man of great wealth who built a bigger barn. What he should have been doing was to say "thank you, God."

Are you actually aware of your greatness? When I say greatness, I do not mean the greatness of the things you possess, not even the abstract truths you think you have learned. But you are great when you have learned to return to the Source that which the Source has given you. Through thanks, return to the Source your whole being, and as you do, you will become aware of your own greatness.

When I was a little boy there was a hymn which began with: "Count your many blessings, name them one by one; and it will surprise you what the Lord has done." I don't know that we are any longer surprised by the good that we have, but certainly it is right to count our many blessings. The blessings that God has for you are not visible to the senses. The real blessings that He has for you is you yourself, living yourself, being yourself, being thankful.

Have you ever noticed how often people count their problems? "I've got this to do and that to do; I've got to take care of things and

I don't know how I'll have time for all of them." Individuals are unconsciously counting their problems or the things they have to do. If you have a problem, be thankful, because in that problem is the gem of your own spiritual greatness if you will but look for it.

It is important to realize that it doesn't matter how the physical body feels, as to whether you can express thanks and be thankful to Him. Sometimes individuals will say: "If I could just get a better physical body I would be able to do better work for mankind," or, "if I had more material abundance," or, "if I didn't have to spend so much time fighting with my neighbor." When these experiences come we use them as opportunities by being thankful that even in the ugly toad there is the precious stone—to use a thought from Shakespeare.

To express thanks you must care for and preserve the whole of God's spiritual creation. This giving of thanks must come from a heart filled with a desire to do something—to care for, to preserve, to love the whole of God's creation. The demand upon you is that your life goes forth as Jesus said to "heal the sick, raise the dead."

"Freely ye have received, freely give." You are to freely give because you have freely received. If you are not giving, but you are rushing around doing a lot of things for other people, that's not necessarily giving. Giving has to come out of your own life. If there is no action as the result of what you think of as your thanks-giving, you are merely expressing a theory about thanks, not genuine thanks; because all genuine thanks lead to action. Thus, thanks-giving must lead to the helping of others who are struggling.

Have you ever thought that the only prayer that God accepts is the prayer of thanks? No matter how good a worded prayer may appear to be, unless it is the prayer of thanks it is not a prayer that God is going to accept.

What then is thanks? It is respect for the whole of God's creation. Respect is thanks-giving for all that the Source has created and has called upon you to share. Be joyously thankful.

XV

AGAIN I SAY - SHARE

Anyone who is starting their adventure in meditation usually sets aside a certain amount of time. And its very easy to believe that meditation is a series of postures, a series of formulas or ways to become still. We think in terms of meditation as merely something that we engage in.

Those who are beginning the adventure of meditation should start there — to find a certain formula, a certain way, a certain means by which to meditate. And meditation can be a great aid to you in eventually coming to that which you find in the quietness of your own Soul. That is the formula which we call meditation, but the meditation that I am talking about goes beyond any formulas.

There is one great difference between the meditation that one engages in as a formula and what I call genuine meditation. The meditation of formula is to get something:

"I want to get still; I want to get quiet enough so I can help the world;" but it's all "getting." In fact, if anyone ever has difficulty meditating it may be that he still thinks of himself as a mortal being still so that he can talk to God, or perhaps that God can talk to him.

God speaks to the meditator who carries his meditation with him every single moment of every single day. It is the meditation of letting God speak, rather than having a group of formulas by which he feels that God will speak to him.

Trying to get one's self in tune with God, with this meditation of formula, or whatever the meditator would call it, may be something in the human experience which may even be very righteous such as getting an understanding of God. But genuine meditation or the meditation of Spirit is a complete surrender of any desire to get anything. It's merely to give one's self away.

Meditation is not setting aside a certain amount of time and feeling that God is going to talk to you at that particular moment. You yourself are the meditation and you are that meditation wherever you are—seeing your Self, living your Self, being your Self at-one with God. Meditation is something that you engage in no matter what you are doing or where you may happen to be.

Spiritual meditation is the meditation where one surrenders himself to the Nothingness of his own soul, because it is in the Nothingness of his own soul that God speaks. It is the meditation of complete surrender of the self to being at-one with the source of Nothingness. The one who has "built many barns," built many formulas of how to meditate or has an accumulation of human knowledge gained from the human mind, finds it difficult to surrender his human knowledge and enter a Realm that is in every sense of the word, a Nothing.

To make a comparison, it is like the blackboard which, if the blackboard is completey filled with writing, a teacher cannot write on it. The blackboard has to be clean. In meditation, God speaks to the "clean blackboard." He speaks to the mind that has nothing written on it. God cannot reach the mind filled with clutter, the mind filled with a preconceived idea as to what God is, a mind endeavoring to "get" something. Of course, I am talking in terms here that do not apply, because God can reach, always.

The meditation I speak of is not the meditation of calming the human mind. It is the meditation that is free from, and not dependent upon the human mind, whether the human mind is calm or not calm. It is the meditation of isolation. It is the isolation of one's self from all confusion, pleasure, harmony or disharmony of the human experience.

The inner kingdom is the kingdom of Isolation— isolation from all knowledge, all knowing, all wanting, all gaining, all kinds of struggle. The inner kingdom is free from struggle, free from striving. The inner kingdom is the kingdom of not-knowing—not the kingdom of knowing. The inner kingdom is the kingdom that is completely free from even the need of the human mind to explain.

Meditation of formula can be physical isolation. Spiritual meditation is spiritual isolation—isolation within and as the spiritual Realm. In this isolated condition of meditation—and by isolated I mean shutting out the problems or solutions of anything in the human experience. In this isolated condition of meditation, the Self observes all that he thought of as outside of himself, as the kingdom within, the inner domain of divine Reality. Meditation is recognizing that one is the spiritual kingdom.

All your decisions should be made from meditation, but not the meditation of: "Now wait a minute—as soon as I have prayed about this I'll give you an answer," or, "When I meditate about this I will make a decision." You have this meditative power with you wherever you are and whatever you are doing. It is through this meditative power that one recognizes that he himself is Spirit-in-action. He is the divine Self. He is the Self isolated from human problems or successes who is actually the observer of the All of spiritual reality. Through spiritual meditation you are enabled to recognize that you are the divine Self who is actually the observer of the allness of divine Reality.

117

In this inner kingdom one realizes that he is not the observer of what the human mind appears to be saying, because he is isolated from what the human mind appears to be saying. He is also isolated from the awareness of the body with its aches, pains and pleasures. He is isolated so that he has in reality no outside environment.

The meditator, in his inner kingdom, has no awareness of an identity as a mere human. Being free from this limitation of being a mere human—or perhaps I should put it the other way around—isolated within his inner kingdom of spiritual Reality, he can be transformed into any form or no form. In this inner kingdom the meditator can experience the transformation of the Self.

When those looking on see what appears to emerge from this meditative experience, emerge from the inner kingdom (although actually I am using words here, because one doesn't really emerge from the inner kingdom), the meditator experiences limited transformation of his inner experience, and can, in limited ways, impart this inner experience to what appears to others as human life. He can bring what he has seen within so that others looking on can feel his guidance.

Depending upon one's ability to communicate, he can share—in a limited way—his inner experience with others. That is, he can share what he has gained from his meditative experience with others. And this is what we call spiritual teaching. The meditator living his meditation is not dependent upon his ability to communicate what he has observed; but the meditator must live and share what he has observed. If he is not sharing his meditation, he is not meditating; because the by-product of all meditation is sharing. One who does not share is one who has not communicated what the Spirit has given him. In short, he has not meditated.

Perhaps you may say: "But what is practical about this? Why is it so important to me?" Being isolated within this inner spiritual kingdom, one can experience the transformation of what appears to those looking on as his outer life. It is a transformation in which others looking on may call healing, reformation and comfort.

The meditator is not limited by what he can or cannot do in the outer world. His sharing is not because he has ability that the human mind says he has (because he is a good speaker or that he is very gregarious and therefore he can meet people)—his sharing has nothing to do with that whatsoever. He shares out of having lived in the inner world. His living and sharing will come from his direct observation of his meditation. He will not be sitting down and saying: "I've got to share something with John Jones—what will I share with him?" And the human mind starts whirling around, trying to find all sorts of abstract or unrelated truths. That's not what a meditator shares. He shares what he first has seen of his inner kingdom through his meditation. He shares what he has first observed in the isolation of the kingdom of Reality.

The meditator has been to the realm of the Unknown and what he has found in that Realm must be respected. He must not then try to manipulate it into a way in which others will accept. He must be very careful that in no way should he try to explain the Unknown. The meditator must live with the Unknown and let the Unknown write upon his "blackboard" that which he must share. His sharing must be the giving of the Unknown to those who may only believe in what they can know.

What I am saying demands an entire change in the way of presenting Truth. If we are not alert we will take the truth that we have gained and then try to bring it down by saying: "Will others understand it?" Others are not obligated to understand the so-called truth that is presented. You are presenting something quite different and the quite different thing that you are presenting is the Unknown. You will present the Unknown out of your freshness and vitality so that those who wish to touch you can be blessed.

Somebody said to me: "Have I made a lot of growth in the last number of years?" And I wanted to say to that individual, but didn't: "There is only one way by which you can calculate your spiritual development and it is by your willingness to share, but not your willingness to share in a group that you feel comfortable with. It is to share where the meditator's observation calls upon you to share. There is no other test needed for your spiritual growth than that of sharing." The meditator is called upon to live in this experience "as he that serveth," as a giver who shares.

You cannot be a sharer, a servant, a giver if you spend your time trying to get somebody else to do your tasks for you. If you say "I wish he or she would just do a little more, then I could have a little less to do!" You are sharing only when you are more concerned about the needs of others than you are about your own needs. You care for the needs of others only as you take everyone into the kingdom with you.

You will never love everyone as long as you try to manipulate yourself into loving others in the human experience. You will love them only through entering the kingdom of Isolation, the kingdom within, the kingdom of spiritual Reality, the kingdom of Nothingness, of no desires, no wants, no personal getting.

Your meditation cannot be a meditation that chooses: "I'm going to love this one and not that one; this one is receptive, but that one is not so I won't bother with that one." You take everyone into the kingdom. You are called upon to serve everyone and you can make no distinction in your service. You cannot decide: this one I'm going to serve; that one I won't serve. To paraphrase a statement in the Bible: "You must eat that which is set before you." The result of all meditation will be sharing and it will be sharing free from personal likes or dislikes.

121

You may say: "But how do you get into this kingdom?" You are not going to get into this kingdom without first coming out. (These are only words, because one doesn't really come out of the kingdom. He is already in the kingdom.) For instance, if you have a pail of water, in order to add fresh water, some of the old water must first be thrown out. But for teaching purposes one can only keep what he gains through his meditation by coming out of his meditation and sharing.

When one observes the Reality of the inner kingdom, the kingdom of the reality of Nothingness, he automatically shares. If one is not sharing he has not been to the kingdom and if he has been to the kingdom he is obligated to share. No one can observe and not share; it is an impossibility. If one is lifted up spiritually, he draws unto him those who would appear to be blessed by his sharing.

One who is not sharing is one who has not really entered the inner kingdom, the kingdom of the Self; because the Self includes every other entity. And because it includes every other entity, for one's own continuous spiritual development, he must share with other identities. The meditator is called upon to go "into all the world, and preach the gospel" of the inner kingdom. He is called upon to heal all manner of sickness and disease—to live a life so close that those in need—no matter where they may be—can reach out and touch him.

The one who would hold the world in the palm of his hand is the one who observes the inner spiritual kingdom, the kingdom of Reality. One is then the sharer of what he has observed in this inner kingdom. He does this sharing free from dependence upon the knowledge of the human mind.

Sharing must be based upon what you have observed through your meditation of the inner kingdom. It must be a sharing given to others because the Source of the inner kingdom has first given to you. Only in the giving to others do you find your Self.

Without sharing there is no genuine spiritual growth. With sharing, the door is open to your continued unfolding of spiritual Reality.

Again—I say, share.

XVI

THE NEW BIRTH

[When this talk was delivered at
TRUTH CENTER, a Universal Fellowship, it
was preceded by the reading of John 3: 1-
15 from the Bible.]

Whether we are aware of it or not,
we are constantly seeing miracles.
Everything around us is a miracle if it is
correctly viewed. Sometimes we wait for a
great miracle to take place; yet we are
surrounded at all times with miracles if we but
have eyes to see.

At our Christening Service I couldn't
help but think again about that wonderful
miracle of a child being born. A miracle! And
then the miracle of a mother's love in caring
for the child, sometimes under very difficult
situations. A miracle! Or just recently as I
was out walking and looked at a beautiful
flower. The flower had colors blended together
and it had a fragrance. A miracle! And how

about the affection which a friend has for a friend—the willingness to sacrifice for a friend. A miracle!

We look for a miracle, but in a very spiritual sense, we ourselves are the miracle. I have used the word miracles, but actually they are mysteries. What is the mystery behind a mother's love? What is the mystery behind the beauty of the flower? What is the mystery that prompts a friend to express his affection to another friend? Mystery! All miracles are mysteries.

We close our eyes to miracles and wait for some far off time when we will see a great miracle, yet we are surrounded by miracles. I could go on citing many other miracles; for instance, the willingness of someone to bite his tongue rather than strike out against another. A miracle, because that's prompted by love.

We try to explain miracles. How often individuals have said to a religious Teacher: "What is a miracle?" If it could be explained it would not be a miracle. Awareness of the divine Source which brings about all miracles must ever remain as a mystery. But do not feel that I am implying that the mystery cannot be "known." The mystery is knowable; but it is knowable only to the "eye" that looks beyond the reasoning of the human mind or what it sees in the sense world.

There are two types of miracles. The ones that you see with your eyes—the miracles that you see around you; and the ones where

you have spiritual Awareness or "eyes to see."
It is not what the human mind says in order to
comprehend those great spiritual miracles, but
the Power behind the thing which you see.

The mystery is not knowable even in the
harmony and order of human life, although the
mystery may point to it. The mystery is
knowable only in the higher harmony and order
of unreasoning Awareness. It is known in the
smallest action of love. In fact, the mystery is
the action of love. If we are to see the holier
mystery, if we are to comprehend that holier
mystery, we must cease looking into the human
mind and even into human acts for the answer
for the reason of living.

Why are we walking through this
experience? For one reason and for one reason
alone — to discover the mystery of life.
Everyone will eventually make that discovery.
But in order to discover this mystery, one must
begin by laying aside his dependence for
knowledge about life on the evidence gained
from the human mind.

We try to find from the human mind why
we live. We look out on human acts and we
say that's why we live. But life is something
much bigger than that. Life is a mystery of
Love being love, expressed by every entity.
We must refuse to accept the mystery of human
living as the only vital mystery if we are to
have an awareness of the genuine mystery—the
mystery of selfless Love actively expressed.
We need no other answer to the mystery of life
because life is the mystery of Love-in-action.

All we need to understand about the reality of life—the reason for existing—is love and faith.

Sometimes we are prone to think that the working of the human mind or the wonders of the material world are the mystery. In one sense they are, but they are not the Great Mystery. We might say that there is a lower mystery and a higher mystery. We have to lay aside the mystery of things we see around us, because eventually that ceases in order that we may gain the eternal Mystery, the mystery of spiritual Love-in-action.

May I encourage you to frequently read the Biblical story of Jesus' encounter with Nicodemus. You recall that the Master told his visitor that he could not enter the kingdom of God (and remember, the kingdom of God is the awareness of one's unity with the divine Source) unless he was "born again." Perhaps Nicodemus thought of that miracle as human birth. Whether he thought of this birth as a miracle or not, he at least wondered just how he could be born again when he was already old.

Nicodemus asked the question: "Can a man enter a second time into his mother's womb and be born again?" Nicodemus saw only the lower miracle—the miracle which is viewed by the human mind and which we call human birth. But there is a greater birth, a greater miracle, a spiritual miracle—the miracle of our awareness of divine Love-in-action.

127

Jesus knew that unity with the divine Source is gained only as we see that which is infinitely more than the reasoning of the human mind. Not in any way am I belittling the reasoning of the human mind. We need it because we have to use it all the time. But the reasoning of the human mind is not the Great Mystery. The Great Mystery is that which we perceive when the human mind is willing to turn aside from mere reasoning in order to perceive and accept the mystery—the Great Mystery—the New Birth.

The New Birth is the lifting up of the view we have of man, of ourselves and of others—in the same way that Moses, centuries ago, "lifted up the serpent." We must look beyond the limited mystery, the mystery of human birth, life and death, and behold the mystery of eternal Life, of selfless Love actively expressed.

Remember Jesus' words: "Except a man be born of water and of the Spirit, he cannot enter into the kingdom of God." We need both, "the water"—to be born with respect for that which is in the human experience; "and of the Spirit"—that which is not of the physical experience.

We need not spend our time denying the lower mystery; we merely look beyond the lower mystery with its absurdities such as love that turns into hate. And certainly hate is a negative mystery. Why do you hate somebody? Why can't you get along with somebody? Why do we war with another nation? That's a negative mystery. We need to be willing to see and to handle, in the only valid way, the so-called "mystery of evil," negative mystery.

We have to look beyond either the positive mystery—the mystery that I referred to as the birth of a life, the beauty of a flower —or the negative mystery, the death of an individual which some would think of as a negative mystery. All the flowers that I looked at the other day probably by now are dead.

We must look beyond the absurdities of the lower mystery, but not in any way criticize, condemn or judge the lower mystery. We must be willing to free ourselves from the materialism that accompanies the lower mystery. We have to let die that which is the important thing or the reality to us. That's what Jesus indicated when he referred to the "corn of wheat," the seed which must fall into the ground and die.

We have to do more than try to seek the mysteries that are to be unfolded to us on a far-off planet—as much as we may feel that that is of some value at the present time. Sooner or later we must see that the seeking of these mysteries often limits us instead of freeing us. We need to reach out in order to accept and live the mystery of divine Love— love lived as spiritual action.

The higher Mystery is the Mystery of spiritual enlightenment which almost all reject.

129

And why do individuals reject these higher Mysteries? They reject them because they do not have eyes to see, the "blessed eyes" which Jesus referred to when he said to his disciples: "Blessed are your eyes, for they see." Individuals must see beyond the limitations that the lower mysteries would present.

We must accept the Light or enlightenment which the blessed eyes see. It is this Light, this enlightenment, which enables us to be "born again," to accept for ourselves and for others the mystery of rebirth. This Light, this enlightenment, this mystery, enables us to be aware—in a sense, to know—that Love is the only way, because God, the governing source, is love.

It is this spiritual Mystery, unknown to human reasoning, which enables us to know and to respect the Godliness in others. To paraphrase some words in John's Gospel: There is no greater love than to lay down your life for another. I would say that there is no greater mystery than love-in-action which prompts you to lay down your life—your self-egotism, your self-centeredness, your self-love —for another.

The mystery of divine Love is always the mystery of sharing—sharing with others. And this sharing of the mystery must be shared self-lessly and impartially. You cannot say: "I have seen the mystery; I respect the mystery, but I can't really learn to love that person or that nation." We have to love—and share. The word love means sharing and there is no love unless it is shared. The Mystery must be shared selflessly and impartially; and we must do this sharing with a sense of confidence. It must be the confidence that the Light of faith has shown us, the enlightenment that is completely devoid of dependence upon the human mind or the evidence of the physical senses.

Think of the greatness that Christ Jesus referred to when he said: "I and my Father are one." It's a mystery most people today wouldn't accept. They would find it very difficult to say "I am one with my Father." Yet you are called upon to live the Great Mystery. That Great Mystery is that you can say and live: "I and the Source which fathers all life for me are one."

What a great and wonderful mystery, the mystery that you and the Source of your being are—and must forever remain—as one. It's almost a mystery too that you can live this mystery and prove it valid right while you appear to be living in the realm of the lower mystery—the mystery that the human mind perceives. But the Light which you love—and which loves you—can enlighten your way every single moment of every single day. In this light of the Mystery—of living life as love—there is no darkness at all.

Eventually everyone will move beyond the darkness of the lower mysteries and have their spiritual eyes opened to behold the divine Mystery. That divine Mystery is oneness with divine Love Itself.

The Mystery is more than just a thing. The Mystery, the great and valid Mystery is you — living at-one with the Source of your being — expressing selfless Love.

The Great Mystery is and ever will be selfless Love actively lived — because you are the Mystery.

XVII

GRACE IS POWER

Grace might be defined in two ways. One of course is the fact that we so often say "grace" before a meal which means we give thanks—a very commendable thing to do. The grace I am going to talk about is another definition of grace.

Grace is the freewill gift of God that comes to you through others. Grace came to others through Christ Jesus and it came to others through other Holy Men who have lived throughout the ages. Grace is God's gift to you—the free generosity of God.

Grace is not a bartered gift where one says, if I give you this then you must give something to me. But grace is the freewill gift, unearned. I often think of a freed slave who had been a slave for forty years and he was asked: What is grace? He said: "Grace is what I should call giving something for nothing." Probably that's as good a definition as you are going to find. It is the giving of something for nothing. In our lives it will be the receiving of unmerited and unearned good.

It's important that we also understand the doctrine of grace. Paul made a doctrine of grace and he calls grace a gift. It is interesting that Christ Jesus does not use the word grace in that sense at all. But Paul in the Bible makes a great point of grace and in all of Paul's writings he begins and ends his letters with grace.

Paul felt that rules, laws and regulations were necessary, but grace is free from rules, laws and regulations. Then you might think that rules, laws and regulations are unnecessary; however they are necessary—they support. As some of you know, I am very fond of sweet peas. Sweet peas need something to grow up on, but you wouldn't say that that which they grow up on are the sweet peas. Of course laws, rules, regulations, tenets and dogmas are what things can grow up on, but they are never the thing itself. The thing itself is love-in-action which is grace.

You will find grace by "touching"* others; you will not find it in any other way. You "touch" the God in others. You're still touching God, but you touch God in another. That is

---

*The words "touch" and "touching" which appear in this chapter are explained later in chapter XXVII.

134

grace coming to you. I realize that this is not the accepted definition of grace, but I would like to broaden that sense of grace for you.

You will never get grace directly, because grace will always come through someone else. You will get grace by seeing God in someone else; and someone else will receive grace by seeing God in you. Grace is someone's love actively expressed. It's that Hindu greeting: "The God in me greets the God in you"—respects the God in you, loves the God in you.

You're going to find grace through another. You're going to find it as the woman in the Bible found that freewill gift through touching Jesus. We have no indication in the story that the woman merited grace at all. Sometimes after I have used that story in a talk or in a class people will say that the woman must have had something that made her prepared to receive her healing. Not so. Grace is unmerited. It is the freewill gift of God given to us at all times whether we humanly merit it or not.

You will never reach the God-power through your own goodness; it will always be the goodness that you see of God in another. The woman touching Jesus didn't receive her healing through her own goodness and perhaps the healing was unmerited. She received the healing through touching the God in Jesus.

God expresses Himself through individuals to bless other individuals. The higher one is in grace, the more pure his grace. The more grace that one expresses, the lower he will be in his own estimation. Grace is not something that builds you up when you say: "I must have a lot of grace because I have a lot of money" or that you have good health. It is the humility or humbleness that indicates your grace.

What is this calling upon you to do? Two things. First, you must give grace; that is, be God-in-action. The other is that you must be willing to receive grace. Let God be so a part of you that others may touch you whether they are worthy or not. The moment you say "This person is unworthy," or "this person isn't ready for the truth," you have shut yourself off from the ability to share your grace. It isn't what another person thinks, nor what another person does; it is what you do. It is the grace or the love which you live for another or others. It is also the grace that you accept from others and accept sometimes from very unusual places.

Be careful that you don't see God in the action such as health or in prosperity, because then you will also have to see Him in what you have as an opposite—when you see an accident. You will have to see God in the accident. If you do, then you will come to the next step. You will say: "Why did God let it happen?" God hasn't anything to do with that. "God is Spirit." God is not that which manipulates man's free will to avoid an accident or something else. God is that which responds to the difficulty—or in some cases He responds even to the over-abundance of good. It is God which feels for the sufferer, but God is not in the suffering. He's not in the accident; He's not in the thing.

Grace is unmerited goodness expressed to an individual. But there is also unmerited evil such as an accident or an illness. Be wary of the thought that when a tragedy comes that you think it's the will of God. It is not God's will, but neither is human prosperity or human well-being or any of the other so-called good things. All these things are the result of man's inherent use or misuse of free will.

Sitting with many people who were in the process of dying, I was very interested to find how many saw an unmerited gift of grace during that experience. They may not have lived a life that was particularly fruitful, but grace was there. They reached out and they touched someone else's love as they made the transition. In some cases it's been my own life they have touched.

You will never find God by taking the safe road, the easy way, getting somebody else to do your tasks for you or avoiding a situation because it is painful. The one who finds the grace of God is the one who exists on the cutting edge of life. All that the safe life can find is a misguided sense of safety; but the one who is willing to live on the cutting edge of life finds a safety, but it's a different safety. It is a safety to explore and to find spirituality.

Aristotle defined the Greek word charis as "helpfulness towards someone in need, not in return for anything." This is as good a definition of grace as can be given. Would you say: "I was good to that person, therefore they should be good to me?" Sometimes parents even fall into this trap. They say: "I was so good to those children as they were brought up; now it's their turn to be good to me!" You cannot work that way. It is giving for giving's own sake.

If you are to experience the saving power of Grace you must avoid self-aggrandizement, self-justification, self-will, self-indulgence. You can never save yourself. Grace is the saving power, the grace you see and accept from another. Grace comes from another, but it is not coming from another person. Grace comes from the God "in" that person. You will never find God in a personal search. You will find God by giving grace and receiving grace, and you're more apt to find your true nature in the grace you receive from others, for it is this grace from others that tells you who you are.

Be willing to "touch" others, especially those whom you think you don't get along with, because they will help you more than those you get along with easily. If you say: "I can't get along with that individual," it may be that the individual whom you can't get along with will be the one who will bring you grace. Or another person says: "I would like to be free from that person who is hating me or misunderstanding me;" but that's not how you

138

should be in contact with that individual. You're not in contact with another person's hating or misunderstanding. You are to be in "contact" with the God in him. You're more apt to find the saving grace in an enemy than in a friend. You're more apt to find it in someone who disturbs you than in one who just lets you sit back and enjoy your own self-indulgence or your self-pity or whatever it may be.

Jesus indicates that we have to love our enemies. We love our enemies because sometimes our enemies will be the very means that will bring us grace. Jesus made this very clear when he said: "Blessed are ye, when men shall revile you, and persecute you, and shall say all manner of evil against you falsely, for my sake." You are blessed when somebody says that to you. You're not blessed when somebody tells you how good you are and how many things you've done for righteous causes and all this stuff. That's not when you are at your greatest point. You are at your greatest point when others criticize and you have so stirred yourself.

The ones who are criticized are more apt to be those who are doing something positive, who are placing themselves on the cutting edge of life. Then Jesus said that the result of this will be that you should "Rejoice, and be exceeding glad: for great is your reward in heaven." You've found grace and you will find it through the persecution, the misunderstanding, the mistrust of those whom you call your enemies. You will not have the saving grace unless you are willing to "rejoice and be exceeding glad."

If you are going to give grace and accept grace you need to be very alert to avoid absolute concepts such as "This is good!" You've seen things that were considered good as a child and now they are not considered good at all. Or the things that were considered bad when I was a child, now are accepted. Avoid absolute concepts of good or bad. Avoid a theory about anything. Use humility. Be willing to be unpopular in this world so that you will receive the grace to inherit the greater world, the world that is not of this universe.

You're not going to find grace by having power or the lack of power. You need to find grace through a new concept of power. You need to ask yourself, what is power? Because what you think is power will tell you a great deal about yourself. Is money power to you? Is a position power to you? Is being part of a powerful nation important to you? If these are powerful to you then that's where you are at this moment.

Grace is free from worldly power. Grace is that freedom to be God-in-action which just freely gives. It is God freely giving. Grace has nothing to do with worldly power, a world church, a powerful organization—a powerful anything—not even the power in numbers. Grace is the stillness of God expressed. It is the simplicity, the humility of God expressed by individuals who have accepted Grace and are now willing to share their grace.

Someone has said that "Grace is nothing if not the final power; and power is force if it is not grace." The power is the power of Grace. When you are prone to think of power, ask yourself, is this the power of Grace or is it human power or the lack of power? You have a right to have, to express and to share the power of grace. As you do, you will see the saving Force expressed in your daily life.

You need, not only to touch others, but to let others touch you. If you are willing to do those two things you will be free from this negative, materialistic power, or more accurately, that which parades as power but is not really power at all.

If you are willing to touch the God in another and willing to let others touch the God in you, you will have a new sense of power, the saving power of Grace.

XVIII

DON'T BE AN "EGO" LISTENER

In his play, "Love's Labour's Lost," Shakespeare makes the statement: "Make passionate my sense of hearing." We need to have a passionate desire to hear, a zeal to hear, a wanting to hear. So often we are so busy talking about truth, talking about God, talking about people that we don't hear. We don't even hear God.

Someone has said that it is not by accident that we are given two ears and one mouth. Would that we would spend more time listening—perhaps twice as much or maybe even more—than we do in speaking. Our speaking should come out of our hearing. We should have a tremendous zeal to hear, to listen. Unfortunately, most individuals think of listening only in terms of what another says to them or what they hear on television or the radio.

In one translation of the New Testament Jesus is quoted as saying: "Take heed how you hear." Are you a "how" listener or a "what" listener? What are you listening to or how are you listening? A good listener is usually very popular, but also he is one who learns a great deal. It's the one who has to do all the talking who gains very little. Haven't you ever been in a conversation when someone says: "Just a minute, I want to say what I have to say!"

How are you going to be a "how" listener? One way is to be attentive. How attentive are you to someone when they talk to you? Do you actually give your all to the listening or are you spending your time thinking: "Now that was very interesting, but what I've got to say is this!" Be a loving listener, not a greedy listener. A greedy listener is one who says: "As soon as he's finished then I'll start talking."

You must learn to be an attentive listener, not a sloppy listener such as giving half of your attention. Maybe you can even go to sleep while the other person is talking. I mean mentally asleep, but also physically asleep, because one hasn't cultivated the ability to listen. The person probably wouldn't go to sleep mentally or physically if he were doing the talking. That is sloppy listening. The disciples went to sleep on Jesus because they could not listen.

Cultivate the "how" listening. If you do, you won't be the "what" listener who says:

"I've heard all that so many times before."
Cultivate not only attentiveness but retention.
You must retain what the person is saying, not
just long enough so that you can answer back,
or so you can get your two cents worth in.
Cultivate the art of listening. As far as the
human experience is concerned, the "how"
hearing has to be cultivated and it has to be
cultivated out of willingness to listen.

If you take heed how you hear, you will
be in control. If you are always thinking about
what others are saying — "I like what that
person is saying! I don't like what they are
saying!"—you've lost your sense of control. If
you are a "what" listener you get disturbed
about wars and rumors of wars, sicknesses,
confusions and often you are overwhelmed by
what you hear. But if you are a "how" listener
you know how to handle what is said.

Above all, don't be a selective listener—
you'll listen to your friends but you won't
listen to your enemies. Maybe it's your enemy
who is going to tell you the most about
yourself. Perhaps you are a "selective"
listener. Do you shut out everything that
disturbs you or anything you don't understand
at the moment, another person's life style or
anything that's conventional? A "how" listener
learns from his listening; a "what" listener
selects only what he wants to hear. You'll
either be a selective listener or you will be a
universal listener and hear in everything
around you, God talking to you, even in the
voice of your enemy.

Are you a listener or a non-listener? A hearer or a non-hearer? What are you hearing? Hearing is an art, an art which must be practiced. Hearing demands that you are concerned more about the needs of others than you are for yourself—for their peace, for their need of food or their lodging. You cannot spend your time thinking that if they were doing such and such they wouldn't be in that position.

Don't be a "turn off" listener; that is, one who turns off anything which is discordant or what one doesn't want to hear. The whole thing can be summed up in that one word, how. How do you listen? Are you a "how" listener? You'll either be a listener or a non-listener. Haven't you ever been with somebody who will turn you off and then they just keep on talking.

A "what" listener is one who listens to what he wants to hear. You've seen that even in people who listen to the same speaker and they all get something entirely different. A "what" listener is also one who is an off-and-on listener. He turns off what he doesn't want to hear and turns on what he wants to hear. There are people who will listen to the type of religious things they want to hear or the world news they want to hear. The interesting thing is that the one who is an off-and-on listener is one who misses the finer things in life. He turns off the music he doesn't like and he can also turn off the voice of God if he doesn't like what God is demanding of him.

145

God speaks directly to us and He speaks to us through others. Sometimes we turn God off and sometimes we turn our fellow man off, but we must remember that both speak to us. We have to be a "how" listener to comprehend what God is saying, whether He's saying it directly to us or through someone else.

There's another listener which we might call the "ego" listener, one who listens only when he is the subject of what is said. Someone may be telling how he built his house and the "ego" listener can't wait to say: "Do you know what I did when I built my house?" And he takes over. The one who talks before he listens is the one who never grows spiritually. An "ego" listener is one who invariably spends his time waiting for another to finish so he can talk.

An "ego" listener, as the term implies, is one who wants to be the center of attention. And this wanting to be the center of attention has given growth to such things as the psychiatrist. Individuals visit a psychiatrist so they can talk about themselves, so that they are the center of attention. It reminds me of that saying of Benjamin Franklin: "Lovers, travelers and poets will give money to be heard." Today we do the same thing. It isn't just the lovers, travelers and poets; nearly everyone does it in some way or another, particularly those who feel the need of going to a psychiatrist. I recall so often in counseling individuals, that they would spend their whole time in talking about themselves. They came because they wanted to be the center of attention.

An "ego" listener is unwilling to listen to the creative thoughts of another. An "ego" listener loves himself. A "how" listener loves others, listens to others. One of the tests of how you love is how you listen, spiritually and affectionately, to others. A "what" listener is one who spends his time talking about his personal background, his feelings, his prejudices and so on. Out of the arrogance of his life a "what" listener invariably is spending his time, rather than listening, in telling others what he has lived, what he is doing.

A "how" listener is not limited by preconceptions. This doesn't mean that you have to agree with everything you hear. But if you are a "how" listener, the listening will perhaps strengthen or modify your own convictions—or even make you think deeper. A "how" listener is willing to listen to even that which is unpopular. He is not limited by what is currently the thing that one is supposed to be interested in.

Is the Christian willing to listen to the Hindu or the Hindu willing to listen to the Christian? If they do, they are "how" listeners. On the other hand if they say: "I have Christianity and that is sufficient," or, "I have Hinduism and that is sufficient," they are "what" listeners.

We have to learn that we are not listening primarily to words, but we have to listen to the sense of the words. A "how" listener is able to go beyond the words, because often an individual cannot put into words what he is really feeling. We have to be able to be a "how" listener so that we can feel the anguish of another which may not be heard in words; or maybe the hope of another, which again, another may not be able to put into words. A "how" listener listens deeply to the concerns, the hopes, the prayers, the desires. Often these are not even voiced in words, yet the "how" listener will hear, for the responsibility for hearing remains with the individual, not with the outside source of hearing another person.

Somebody once asked me what I considered to be a great person—how would I know a great person. And I can remember saying, without any hesitation, that it would be how he listens. I haven't changed that concept even though the question was asked many years ago. One's greatness is measured by his ability to listen, how he listens. But if it's what he listens to he will only hear the words, which he will then either accept or reject according to his preconception.

Hearing others is a fine thing to do, but you must also hear your Self. You must become so convinced that there is the divine Power talking directly to you that you will hear that inner Voice. A "how" listener is one who listens to the inner Voice, whether it is expressed directly to him or whether it appears to come through another.

In our daily experience we have to remember that we are all part of the Whole. We are part of the spiritual universe and therefore, we are all communicating with one another. It is important to realize that God communicates to you through what others say to you. Cultivate your ability to hear with your "blessed ears," your spiritual ears.

We hear physically with our physical ears, but it's obvious that there is—and there must be—that spiritual ear which "hears" the word of God. Christ Jesus demanded a higher sense of listening when he said: "Blessed are your eyes, for they see: and your ears, for they hear." We need to cultivate those spiritual ears, the "ears that hear," the ears that God, the divine Source has created.

In Proverbs it says: "The hearing ear, and the seeing eye, the Lord hath made even both of them." Do you listen in such a way that you are hearing God speak to you because you have the "hearing ear?" A "how" listener is one who listens to God within himself; and only as he is willing to listen to God within himself will he really be able to listen to others. In short, he will have the "blessed ears." (Blessed are your ears for they hear.) The "blessed ears" are the "how" ears.

This talk began with a quotation from Shakespeare's "Love's Labour's Lost" and I think these words could be used as a prayer. In that play, Shakespeare puts into the mouth of one of the characters these words: "Bestow on me the sense of hearing." I might add: Bestow on me the "how" of hearing.

XIX

RELIGION ON THE MOVE

John Montgomery, in his work, "The Pillow," writes: "A friend to him who has no friend—Religion." You are religious when you are a friend to him who has no friend. Religion is not a group of teachings about God or man's relationship to God, but genuine Religion is service. It is friendliness to the unfriendly.

Religion—what does the word mean? To go to the root meaning doesn't tell us very much. In fact it's of very little help. There's no Greek or Roman word which corresponds exactly to our English word religion, so we need to look deeper. Even a dictionary might give you a meaning such as "Concern over what exists beyond the visible world, differentiated from philosophy in that it operates through faith." A good definition, but it's only part of religion as I use the term.

The teachings of religion and the teachings of church should be the same; but I would like to make a distinction that is actually a solecism in language because no distinction can be made—or should be made. For teaching purposes I would like to separate religion from church and church from religion. When I talk about church I mean church organization, not churchly people.

Release any thoughts you may have about religion as being a set of rules, regulations or teachings. Lift it above philosophy, which of course is reasoning without God. And think about some of the teachings of the traditional church which keep us from finding out what religion really is.

One of the teachings of the traditional church is that the purpose of religion is to bring comfort. But this is not the purpose of religion. You have it in such statements as: "If you were thinking religiously you would have peace of mind." This teaching dilutes the genuine purpose of religion, because religion is not to find something for one's self, but to give one's self away. So often we say: "All is perfect, all is good and everything will work out." This dilutes the great purpose of religion.

Another thing that deprives one of the genuine concept of religion is the sense that religion is to bring piety—if you live a pious life, you live a good life. What comes with it usually is self-righteousness.

151

The third is what I would call "suburban thinking." I don't know that there is such a thing, but it is the thought where we get into a suburban idea of "everything being comfortable." You have the "comfortable pew" where you can sit back and just get comfortable. Actually, we should be made uncomfortable by religion. We should see that we are not fulfilling our sense of service to others. We should replace the solemn services with the genuine sense of service to others. And we should replace this "suburban thinking," this thinking of "what is good for me," with the sense of world service, universal service, universal thinking.

Church—as I am using the word—is not to be confused with Religion. Religion is fundamentally a call for service, a call for interdependence of every one of God's creatures on every other one of God's creatures. Unfortunately the church too often has segregated church. They say "my denomination as opposed to this denomination;" or "Christianity as opposed to Hinduism." Genuine Religion teaches interdependence of all in God's universe. Churches, church organizations must become religious. Often they are very unreligious, intolerant. We don't see the bigness of Religion. We don't see the call of Religion for our interdependence.

Religion is that which demands reformation within the individual. Religion is that which calls for the individuals who are religious to transform the world by lives of selfless service. Religion is that which calls upon those who believe they are religious to transform their lives through selfless service. It is the religious person who is leading the world out of its limitations.

If you want a definition of what a religious individual is like, I suggest that you go to the Beatitudes. This is what a religious person is. He is the "poor in spirit"—not the rich one who is trying to make a demonstration of more goodness for himself. He is the one that is mourning because he realizes he is not giving the fullness of his spirituality to the world. He's the meek—not the one who can conjure up a great military force to uphold his will. The religious one is the one who is hungry and thirsty to do right, to live right, to live the religious life. The religious one is the one who is merciful and shows mercy to everyone, especially to those who persecute him. Above all, he is pure in heart; that is, he is not getting down into the impurity of hatred. Such a one is a peacemaker.

Some individuals include what follows as one of the Beatitudes, some do not. "Blessed are they which are persecuted for righteousness' sake: for theirs is the kingdom of heaven. Blessed are ye, when men shall revile you, and persecute you, and say all manner of evil against you falsely, for my sake." What are you to do? What is the religious individual doing? He rejoices and is exceedingly glad because he knows that great is his reward in heaven. This is the part that is not always included as part of the Beatitudes and yet it is the summary. It is doing all these things that have been listed above when you are persecuted. I defy anyone who does all these things to go out and blow up an airplane or to have an armada of airplanes dropping destruction upon another. I defy anyone who is taking this seriously to do any of this.

"Blessed are ye, when men shall revile you, and persecute you, and shall say all manner of evil against you falsely" because you live the religious life. "For my sake" is to live the religious life. "Rejoice and be exceeding glad: for great is your reward" in the heaven of your own being.

Religion is that which brings an awareness of the necessity of Christly service —and especially when one is persecuted. In that passage it says "for my sake"—an idiom which means doing what a spiritual Teacher has demanded. What does Christ Jesus or any valid religious Teacher demand? He demands selfless service. Religion then is that which demands daily activity, daily service. Religion is not leisure-time that we give when we pray. Religion is something we live, that we are—not something that makes us comfortable because we went to a service on a Sabbath day. It's that which challenges us to do something. It is that which challenges us to enter the Realm of spirituality.

Frequently the churches have become irreverent, as far as the activities around them are concerned. We must watch that in our activities we don't become irreverent, because what we have is something very vital. Religion is leading, but so often the churches are following. Above all, we find that churches are very tardy in action. The churches should be the ones that are leading in finding solutions to race relations and in finding solutions to war. They should be leading in providing sanctuary for the poor, the sick and the suffering. The churches must become religious, and not religious in their definition of religion, but religious in the sense of selfless service. Too often churches have become bankrupt in their service.

It has been a tragedy that so often church organizations have been those that follow; whereas, Religion leads. For instance, church organizations so often follow race relations. We've seen it within the last hundred years that many times it has been the church that has resisted the sense of finding a unity between the races. It is the churches which uphold war and we find religious thinkers upholding war. They will say that it is perfectly right to have warlike action or place a racial limitation on an individual.

Watch that we do not become tardy. Have you ever thought that when we become tardy in our action, we are becoming a church person? When we are not at the situation before the situation happens and we try to put things together after an event, we are acting like a church. So often a church is only active after public opinion or social organizations have already moved forward and taken care of the situation. Religion is moving before; churches too often are followers. Religion is not following, as church organization is. Religion is on the move. Religion is God in motion. One who is religious has to be willing to move in accordance with God's forward motion. It's "In him we live, and move, and have our being."

How often individuals say: "I like the old songs." There's nothing wrong with that. But don't like them to such an extent that you can't take the new songs. Or, "I like the old way of doing things!" Ask yourself: "Am I holding on to the status quo in anything in my life? Or am I willing to move? I like this type of art, but I don't like that type of art. I like to hear this person talk, but I don't like to hear that person talk." There's nothing wrong with that, but don't like it to such an extent that you can't move, because movement is going to be demanded of the religious individual. Religion teaches of the God of motion, of movement. "In him we move!"

Churches need to become religion-in-action. What we have failed to realize is that the religion of Jesus and other spiritual Teachers are revolutionary teachings. They demand that one love when there's hatred; going to the one in prison when the person in prison may not be socially accepted; caring for the sick; doing some thing. It is not turning the teaching around and becoming a church activity in which you say: "I'm making myself more comfortable."

Genuine Religion is a rebellion against church ritual. So often a church has hidden behind its church teaching and tenets and it has done this instead of engaging in what can be called social action. The religious view that Jesus presented was in conflict with the organizational view of his time; and religion today is still in conflict with the organizational, religious view of the churches, its tardiness and its personal sleaziness. Churches get settled in their ways and they say: "This is the way we have always done it!"

One time when I was called to conduct some church services there was one member of the church who had always dominated the person who conducted the services in that particular church. Some members said I was going to have a difficult time because after the first service she would tell me what I did wrong. Sure enough, after the first service, this lady who was a member and was very wealthy and had contributed extensively financially to the church came back and said: "It was a good service but, but, but..." and she went through three or four buts that she thought should be changed. I listened to her and then I said, "How much confidence do you have in me?" And she said: "I have great confidence in you."

Then I said: "I appreciate your coming back to speak to me. Will you express that confidence in knowing that now that you have mentioned these things to me that I will take them to God and God will tell me what to do— and I will do what God tells me to do." Before I said that I prefaced my remarks by saying: "Will you do just one more thing for me?" When I look back on the situation I realize that when I asked her to do one more thing she thought I was going to ask her to help, as the others who had conducted a service in that church had always done.

She looked at me and said, "Oh, yes, I'd be glad to do anything." Then I said: "Will you have enough confidence in me to know that I will go to God and that whatever God tells me to do I will do." For a moment she looked stunned. And then she said: "You know, I like that!" I never heard from her in the next three years when I served in that church.

What was the religious service that Jesus demanded? Did he demand that we be person pleasers or group pleasers? Or did he demand that we serve, regardless of whether we please other people? We have to watch that we don't become person pleasers. Too often church organizations have been nothing more than just person pleasers. They will take care of the wealthy member or the educated one and forget the poor. Or there will be a little group and that little group will get along becoming weak instead of strong. Religion must be a strong and vital thing.

If you've studied church history, it's rather interesting how many churches started with a wonderful vision. After a few decades—and sometimes a lot less than that—instead of becoming a vision that moves, churches become a protection in a particular way of thinking, acting, living. They lose the God of vision, they lose the God of movement. Churches invariably lead to stagnation and the ones who support churches invariably become stagnant individuals.

The difference between church organization and religion is that church has based what it teaches on belief; whereas, religion bases its demands upon faith. A church will say: "You've got to believe in God." That wasn't really God. That God must die so that you can have the God of faith. So often people will get up-tight when they hear the saying that God must die, because they think that they're talking about God dying. They're talking about a belief in a God of superstition, of punishment, of all the things that churches have so often talked about. That belief has to die in order that you can find the true God, the God of faith—faith lived in the heart and in one's life.

The God of most churches will have to die. And why will it have to die? Because that God never lived. That God was a God of hatred, sometimes a God of punishment. That God must die because it never was a God. The God that churches have taught upholds racism or upholds the status quo—or something of that nature. That God will die only as one becomes awake to the God of religion. That church God is already dead.

Ask yourself: "Am I willing to let my church God die?" Until you are able to let your church God die you can't have the God of Jesus, the God of religion. Because the God of religion is the God of service, of doing, of experiencing, of going to the prison, of caring for the sick, of loving one's enemies.

The church God is "up there" looking down from a throne or something. I became so aware of that kind of thinking the other day at a funeral service. The minister kept talking about those who were sitting on the right hand of God and that all these people (he specified those who had not found Jesus Christ), those masses that are going to be in Hell! And I thought the most populated place will be Hell. Why? Because they have a God, but they are separated from their God, trying to find God. That God "up there" never lived.

The church God is an absent God, whom you have to call on to come and help you. The religious God of Jesus is that where he was, God was; that where you are, God is. It is the religious God which Jesus defined as "The kingdom of God is within you." You're going to have to find that God within. That God, the God of religion, lives in your heart and in your life.

The church God is so often the God that is separated from you and from your service. The religious God is the God within which expresses Himself through your service and appears both within and without. When Jesus said "the kingdom of God is within you" he did not mean there is something within you as opposed to out there. It is within, expressing itself as without.

Religion is faith in the "Other World," the kingdom that Jesus talks about when he says that the kingdom is not of this world. Religion is that which encourages faith in the

"Other World" made manifest in this world as service.

Church organization is so often secular; whereas, Religion is for all. It's a tragic thing that traditional Christianity and its churches appear to be declining. We shouldn't be disturbed by that, because genuine Religion, the Religion that Christ Jesus and other spiritual Teachers have taught, will be forever available to guide and to guard those who are religious. When I say those who are religious I mean those who are engaged in selfless service.

What is your real religious purpose for existing? Perhaps it has never been given any better than the way Jesus put it when he said: "I am among you as he that serveth." This is the over-riding reason for religion—to provide service, because a religious individual is one who is serving in this world. Service—and only this service—is the real purpose for religion and religious teaching. One who is religious does not seek to be understood. He doesn't even seek to get his church teachings across. He is engaged in living his life as Christly service.

That wonderful 13th chapter of First Corinthians starts off with a definition of what we could define as church—"speaking with the tongues of men and of angels." Churches say: "We're speaking for the angels, we're speaking for good!" What the writer of this passage is saying is that even if you do speak with churchly wisdom, you haven't Religion unless you have a sense of service.

161

Religion then is that which is showing what love is, how love can be put into service, into action. It's doing even more than that, it's demanding that love must be put into action.

In 1611 when the King James Version of the Bible was compiled, the word charity meant love put into action. Religion is that which calls for the putting of love into action.

XX

THE GREAT NEED

The great problem in the world today is that there is not enough love shared. There's not enough love shared wholeheartedly and freely. It's foolish to seek opportunities to share love, we just have to share love with everything that comes into our experience.

The great need is for love to be lived, but we cannot gain the ability to love; we cannot understand why we should love; we just love. Love is not something that you put on at certain times and then express love. Selfless love is what you are, being shared freely, joyously and abundantly.

This selfless love never requires that the one who is to be loved must return love. That would not be love. Selfless love never seeks a reward for its giving. Selfless love means that one finds his own identity, his own reality, his own purpose for living in the joy that he has given to the one loved.

Love is to be shared selflessly with no thought of how or what one is going to get back from that love. Such love can bless the one to whom the love is given, only if the receiver of the love accepts it selflessly. But the one giving the love cannot spend his time thinking whether that other person is going to accept the love selflessly.

Genuine Love demands that in willing to be loved selflessly one must become part of the God-power that has prompted the giver of the love to share selflessly. Selfless love is to be given, but selfless love is also to be received. Love can be kept only in giving it away and by the willingness to accept love.

Have you ever thought how much importance Christ Jesus placed on that little word love? His instructions to his disciples were to "Love one another; as I have loved you." Notice that there are two parts to the statement. He had loved. He had shown by example out of his own experience, out of his own life, out of his own living what love was; and he said to his little band of followers "love one another." Why did Jesus make this demand on the disciples? Because one proves one's discipleship only through love lived.

We need to understand the importance of love and love in our daily life. Our lives must become lives of love lived. Could the reality of what Jesus taught be made practical in the lives of his disciples? Indeed, Love is the only practical force. And Jesus understood that all that he had given his disciples would vanish away if they did not love.

If you believe that your love has lessened, it indicates that you have not really loved. You must give your love away. You cannot start by saying: "If I love myself first then I'll be able to love." But loving yourself is not genuine Love, because Love that parades as self-satisfaction is a pale counterfeit for genuine, spiritual Love. If one loves out of his own self-satisfaction because it gives him pleasure to love, such so-called love eventually becomes indifferent. It can even become hatred—not only of one's self but hatred for one's neighbor for whom the love appears to have been expressed. Hatred isn't a practical force at all; it always has repercussions.

Selfish love—that is, love we give with the hope of getting something back (and of course selfish love is really a solocism in language)—brings no lasting joy. But genuine joy is found in unselfed, spiritual Love. This love is shared freely and without thought of whether the individual is worthy of the love that is expressed towards him. We must share love and there never can be an ending to such sharing. The only thing that is permanent is love shared.

Sharing is the inner life of Spirit expressed in what is thought of as the outer life. The inner life of Love must express itself in what we think of as the outer life. The great demand which God, divine Love, places on each of us is that we share. What do we share? We share ourself. It is this selfless sharing of ourself which is being love-in-action.

165

Anyone who is not sharing with others has not found spiritual Love. Only as we share with others, that is, only as we love others do we truly love ourselves. It's not the other way around. It's not finding the love of ourselves first so we can share, but Love is sharing with others; and through this sharing—seeking first the kingdom of God, the kingdom of Love—we are able to share.

Selfless love cannot be divided so that you can give your love to one individual but not to another. You cannot divide love and say: "I will give love to my nation, but I will withhold it from another nation;" or, "I will give it to this political party but I will withhold it from that political party." You do not divide your love by giving only part of it away. I realize that I am talking about a paradox, because in giving love away you give all of it away. And in the giving of it away you also keep all of it.

Spiritual possessions are retained through the giving of them away—and only through the giving of them away. Material things—you give them away and you no longer have them. If I give someone my coat, I no longer have my coat. But with spiritual things this is not so. Spiritual things must be given away, must be shared if they are to be kept and if they are to grow. If I have five dollars and I want to share it with five people I would have to give each one a dollar. But not so with spiritual qualities which can be given in their total to every individual. And in the giving of them in their total we prove our spiritual perfection.

If a mother has four children in a family she cannot say she is going to give just so much love to each child. It's true that she may only be able to give so much time to each child, but she does not have to divide her love. Love can be given in its total to all the children. If you diminish love by splitting up the parts, you weaken love; you also diminish the joy of love. Love is giving in its total.

How do you love? You love by identifying yourself and your identity with another self and identity. Love is not giving part of yourself away, love is sharing your whole self with another. I still remember a young couple who came to me a number of years ago for consultation and they were having matrimonial problems. I had conversations with them individually and I eventually had conversations with them together. In the individual conversations they both said something to the effect that they had gone into the marriage on a fifty-fifty basis. When I had the visit with them together I said: "That's your problem, because you cannot go into marriage on a fifty-fifty basis." Love demands the giving of one hundred percent to the one loved.

They began to love the other individual a hundred percent, not holding back fifty percent for one's self, but giving away one's whole being — being willing to sacrifice one's own identity, if necessary, on a cross, as Jesus did for another. The matrimonial difficulties disappeared, because they were seeking their own in one another's good.

It is important to understand that spiritual Love is always disinterested as to how another accepts the love. Love gives love just for the sake of giving love, not to see how the one loved will return love. One who truly loves is not ever interested in how another responds to the love given. He just loves and loves selflessly.

Selfless love seeks its own perfection in the good received in the sharing. Selfless love does not demand the satisfaction of looking on the one that had been loved and seeing how much good he has given to that individual. He finds satisfaction through the giving of love and not in the by-product of that love.

The joy of love is not found in the effects of love—how the other person responds to love or the conditions that are changed. The joy of loving is found in the loving itself. Such love seeks but one thing, the good of the one loved. Seeing the by-product of such loving, the selfless lover leaves it for others to see; but the selfless lover does not think about the by-product.

Love makes no comparisons between love given and love received. Love is love, whether it appears as love given or love received. Such giving and receiving of selfless love is the only genuine proof that one has gained a measure of perfection.

Selfless love expressed is in itself spiritual strength. It sees what another needs and calls forth from himself, from his true identity, from his spiritual development, the spiritual strength to care for the needs that have been manifested. All genuine strength is to be found in selfless, spiritual Love actively expressed. It is "not by might, nor by power, but by my spirit," the word of the Lord, expressed through sharing.

Christ Jesus and all spiritual Teachers have demanded of their disciples (and that is the demand of the strength of love) that they have the strength to love and that they have the strength to go into the world as selfless love. Selfless love shared will always be accompanied by the strength that goes into all the world to preach the gospel, to heal the sick, to go to the prison.

One who has grown spiritually finds his satisfaction in selfless service to his God— expressed through selfless service to God's creatures and creation.

Sharing God's love is living the spiritual life.

XXI

THE LOOKING IN ADVENTURE

Whether we realize it or not, we're taking part in a new adventure or readventure. This adventure takes place in the heart and the spirit of the spiritual man; and everyone is engaged in this adventure. It is the quest to find what has validity, what is real.

While we talk about an adventure, we are actually talking about a rediscovery, a search for validity as to why we live. The adventure we take part in is the adventure of finding the very essence of being.

We cannot take part in this adventure by just analyzing what the human mind tells us. We can never take part in this adventure by merely questioning the human mind and what the human mind has to say about man and the universe. We have to see with spiritual eyes and let these spiritual eyes guide us in our adventure. We have to hear with spiritual ears and let the leadings that we have gained from this hearing guide us.

Correctly viewed you are your own adventure. It is not "looking out" to find the adventure, but it is "looking in," for the adventure will be within yourself. You must begin your adventure by burying your present limited view of Divinity—not looking for God "out there" some place. Your adventure must start by looking within yourself, within your spiritually God-created nature to find Him.

Everything that you need to know—all the enlightenment that you need to know about the spiritual nature of God, man and God's universe is to be found within. That which will enlighten you on your adventure is not without, it is actually within. Or perhaps, more accurately, you are the Light of your own adventure.

We may believe that we are seeking the God of reality and I suppose in one sense we are. But actually it is the Light within which illuminates our awareness of that which is actually happening—as God unfolding Himself through us, in us and as us.

The adventure is ours, but the reality or the seeking is not, because the Reality has already been created. We may believe that we seek it, but in reality it has already been created and is in existence. The adventure is the unfolding of this already existing Reality.

171

We must be more than spectators looking out upon Reality. We are not spectators looking out. All that is real, genuinely real, is within ourselves. The adventure is becoming aware of ourselves as the Reality. We must dedicate and perhaps rededicate ourselves to the genuine Reality of our own eternal, spiritual existence.

In reality, your adventure is not in seeking God, but responding to the ever-availability of God seeking you. What you are called upon to engage in is the discovery and rediscovery of the actual nature of God, which God is ever revealing to you—as You.

God is already kingdomed within you. Jesus put it so well when he said: "The kingdom of God is within you." Then your adventure must always be an inward quest. It is the inward quest of discovering God which is kingdomed, that is, living within you. Within you, view the whole of the universe of Spirit. Within you, view the source of divine Spirit Itself.

In order to take part in this adventure we need to view man and the universe as the creation of God; and the adventure is the rediscovery of the nature of God and the unity of all that God has created, man and the universe. This is why it is necessary for us to start by recognizing the God in another before we try to find the God in ourself.

Man in his scientific wanderings through life believes that he has created the universe

172

out of his own limited and limiting knowledge. He believes that everything around him has been the creation of his own enlightenment— even the trees. He feels that in some place man planted a tree; therefore there's a tree. He looks out at his house and says "I built the house." And this may even seem to be true in the human experience. But in "the Other" kingdom, where the true spiritual adventure takes place, there is the divine Source that is the creator.

In his Sermon on the Mount, Christ Jesus said: "Ye have heard that it hath been said, Thou shalt love thy neighbour, and hate thine enemy. But I say unto you, Love your enemies, bless them that curse you, do good to them that hate you, and pray for them which despitefully use you, and persecute you."

Here we have a definition of what genuine adventure is. It is loving, blessing, doing good and praying for others. Through service to others we take part in the divine adventure of learning the nature of God, of spiritual man and of God's spiritual universe.

Including your enemies in your love blesses both you and those whom you previously thought of as your enemies. Not only must you include your enemies, you must include your friends; all that you have thought of as nature; and all that you have thought of as the animal world—as part of your own individual nature.

You must see everything—your enemies, your friends, your family, all that you have previously believed to be "out there"—as within your own spirit, the spiritual nature of all that is "out there." This is why it is so important that you keep in mind that you are called to love, to bless, to do good, to pray for others, especially your enemies. The misadventure in life is to hate. Whenever we hate we are keeping ourselves from the great adventure that God has for us as we walk through this experience.

The great adventure is obedience to the Golden Rule, doing unto others as we would have them do unto us. The Golden Rule is the rule by which you find your spiritual nature; and your search cannot be separated from obedience to the Golden Rule. "All things whatsoever ye would that men should do to you, do ye even so to them." You cannot have your spiritual nature separated from your service to others. Doing righteously to others is being righteous to yourself.

Doing unto others includes not only man, but also animals and nature—and doing unto others is doing unto yourself. Blessed are you if you are taking part in the adventure of including all in your love, including that which you have thought of as "the Other," out there.

We must realize that this is not an external adventure that we are going to engage in. The adventure is looking to the higher Source, to "the Other" kingdom, the kingdom that Christ Jesus assures us is not of this world.

You are not an isolated identity. In all of God's creation there is no such thing as an isolated identity. You are one with all spiritual identity—hence, your "within-ness" includes "the Other." It includes the without as within.

The search within is not a self-centered quest. The search includes all that you may previously have believed to be "out there" in some other place. That "out there" must become an "in here" experience. Everything "out there" has to become an inner experience, especially at the beginning of your spiritual adventure.

Within yourself, within your awareness of the reality of God, you must include "the Other," whatever "the Other" is in your experience.

You must remember to love "the Other," to bless "the Other," do good to "the Other," to pray for "the Other." For whether you are aware of it or not—at this moment, "the Other" is you, as much as you are "the Other."

XXII

THE MOTHER WITHIN YOU
(A Mother's Day Message)

Those of us who have had happy and constructive experiences with our mothers like to think back from time to time of just what constructive motherhood is. Recently in thinking about this, I recalled a passage by Christ Jesus which said: "Whosoever will save his life shall lose it; but whosoever shall lose his life for my sake and the gospel's, the same shall save it."

Perhaps this thought of losing one's self in service to another is the very best definition that one can have as to what motherhood is. A mother finds her life saved in the ratio that she loses herself in service to her child or children.

We're in a society in which we talk constantly about gaining, yet there is also constructive losing. We need to learn the constructive use of losing. We lose ourselves to find ourselves. There's no such thing as finding one's self through a manipulation of right thinking, of gaining a position or anything else. We gain ourselves through losing ourselves in service to others. The reason for this of course is quite simple—we're part of the Whole. And in losing ourselves to the Whole, we find ourselves.

In most religions motherhood is honored. In the Bible mothers were the most honored women; and great emphasis was placed in the Bible and other great religious writings on the influence for good of mothers. It's rather interesting that in the Book of II Chronicles the expression: "And his mother was" is used about twenty times. This is used to show the importance that the writer placed upon the influence for good that mothers can express.

In Ezekiel it says: "As is the mother, so is her daughter." Hebrew women, especially mothers, were a symbol of love. Hebrew women loved their children; and the Hebrews of Bible times had the deepest respect and reverence for mothers. It's rather interesting that the words mother and mothers are used some 300 times in the Bible. So we readily see the great respect that the Bible writers had for motherhood. While the Bible writers had a great respect for mothers, their society was primarily a man's world, a male oriented society; and this continues almost until the present day.

Too often we think of mothers as merely one of the functions that women are expected to perform if they are to live a full and rounded life, failing to realize that women have a much greater and more varied role, of which motherhood is but one facet. Yet we must not lose the great importance of the symbol of motherhood. Mothers give birth, sometimes at great inconvenience to themselves—sometimes even in giving up their own life for the child. A mother cares for the needs of her growing

177

offspring; and this is done in both the physical realm and emotional realm.

Until quite recently a woman was considered to be a person who was to live at home, raise children and provide a home for the bread-winner. While I would not in any way belittle the greatest gift that a woman can give to the world—bringing a child into the world—we must realize that women are entitled to more than mere reverence. They are entitled to more than just thinking of themselves as mothers.

Even today the status of women is low—religiously, socially and legally. We must realize that we have a duty to help women emancipate themselves from being considered inferior; not to be equal with men, but to be their own identity. In recent years, probably in this decade there has been some change, but even greater change is needed.

What is needed is not so much the talking about women's rights as it is to express, each of us individually, the spiritual concept of womanhood. Jesus said we should "worship the Father in spirit and in truth." The same is true of worshiping the Mother "in spirit and in truth."

We do not want to lift women merely over to where they become "like" men, but we want them to find their status as a complete entity. Just as men must find their status as complete entities, in which they express not only what they think of as masculine qualities, but also feminine qualities. We must recognize that women have a right to express the qualities we think of as masculine as well as the feminine qualities.

We need to do more than just move across the line of human behavior. We need a whole new spiritual concept. We must raise our concept of womanhood to the spiritual Realm. We need a new view of motherhood where we find birth, growth and everything as a spiritual activity, controlled by and expressed through spiritual development.

Jesus refers to the "Father in me." We should also recognize the Mother in every individual—in you and in me. He said: "I am in the Father, and the Father in me." You could also say "I am in the Father and the Father in me," and "I am in the Mother and the Mother in me."

While Jesus does not talk about God being feminine as well as masculine, certainly he had a purer view of the Father as spirit and also of Mother as spirit. On one occasion he indicated that those who were his followers were those who loved and lived both the fatherhood and motherhood of God.

A human love of father or mother is not sufficient. In fact, Jesus goes so far as to say that he that loveth father or mother more than what I stand for is not worthy of "me." The passage in the King James Version of the Bible reads: "He that loveth father or mother more than me is not worthy of me." And the "me" of

179

course is what he taught—his love, his spirit, his truth, his faith. Anyone who places human love above that great spiritual Love is not worthy of what a spiritual Teacher is giving.

Most individuals restrict their love merely to the love they find in the human experience. Love turns into hate, distrust, jealousy or something else. The love that is needed is spiritual Love, the Love that is found in the realm of divine Spirit, controlled by the Father-Mother Spirit.

All genuine religious Teachers demand more than just finding the Spirit within. It is finding the Spirit as God, as the Father-Mother within. The Father in you, the Mother in you is what is demanded of you to express. You are called upon to live the Father as strength, courage and perseverance and to find that in your Self as the God within you. You are also called upon to live the Mother as love, tenderness, compassion and to find that Mother within you.

XXIII

THE TEMPLE OF SPIRIT

[When this talk was given at TRUTH CENTER, a Universal Fellowship, it was preceded by the reading of a brief passage from the Gospel of John 2: 13-16. "Make not my Father's house a house of merchandise."]

The Jews of Jesus' time were still practicing in the temple, animal sacrifice such as sheep, oxen, doves. And they were exchanging money at the entrance to the temple because they could only contribute money of a certain coinage. There were money lenders who were making great sums of money by forcing individuals to exchange their Roman money for money that would be acceptable by the temple.

We only have to look around to see how often the Lord's house is made a house of merchandise. It's interesting, that word merchandise, because we see everything merchandised. We even see political candidates merchandised—much as you would merchandise a bar of soap. We see religion merchandised. Look at TV preachers who are trying to induce people to contribute large sums of money. They're selling religion and in doing so they are basically violating one of Jesus' basic instructions: "Freely ye have received, freely give."

Jesus' teaching, "Make not my Father's house a house of merchandise," is practical today. We are not to merchandise. Then what are we to make His house? It's to be made as a house in which love is taught and lived. Is our house a house of merchandise, a house of just mere lip service? We are to make it so inclusive as Spirit in operation that it becomes the avenue through which selfless service to others is expressed.

If you're not going to make the Father's house a house of merchandise, what are you going to make it into? Jesus said: "God is Spirit: and they that worship him must worship him in spirit and in truth." In this statement he defined God anew. Then the house of worship has to be a house of Spirit. It has to be that which is beyond anything material—beyond merchandise. It has to be the kingdom that is "not of this world," the world of merchandise.

"Make not" corrupts. Don't corrupt "my Father's house." We are to make our Father's house a house of great freedom so that others and ourselves can be what God has created us to be. We are not to make "perverse disputes" as part of that house, where we dispute with others as to what the teaching of the church is.

"Perverse disputes" are words that Paul uses in one of his letters to Timothy. A house of merchandise invariably becomes a house where we argue about the teaching. We engage in perverse disputing. The true church is a church which enables us and encourages us to accept the teachings. It is not a limiting thing, it is a freeing experience. The church is not that which engages in disputes, but the spiritual church is that which frees us from disputes, from disputes even from those who think and act quite differently than we do.

Paul's instructions were to "withdraw thyself" from "perverse disputings of men of corrupt minds." The spiritual church is that which frees one from the man of corrupt mind. Watch that you don't think that man of corrupt mind is someone else. Maybe it is, but it's more likely to be yourself. You are the man that you have to free yourself from—from the corrupt mind, the corrupt teaching, the teaching that bigness is greatness, that Spirit can be merchandised. It can't! The house of God is free from merchandising, from that which corrupts men's minds.

The corrupt mind often parades as church. Listening to the disputes of the men of corrupt minds invariably leads to disputes. Or to state it more accurately—it is the disputing itself. So many of the great wars, so many of the divisions among men—even up to today—have been caused by corrupt minds parading as church, saying this is the way religion is to be interpreted. The church of Spirit must be more than a house of merchandise. The church of Spirit must be found within, which frees one from the opinions of the corrupt mind—your own or another's.

Churches very frequently argue about the meaning of something, and in so doing, make God's house a house of merchandise. When I say a house of merchandise I mean "something" which churches make into "something" rather than an inner force that demands spiritual redemption and calls forth the higher nature, the spiritual nature of an individual.

How many disputings do we still hear about, such as the nature of heaven, when the Second Coming is going to take place or what is a moral issue? All of this parades as if it were a part of church; and it has absolutely nothing to do with the church. That is the house of merchandise. It merchandises a teaching about heaven, a teaching about the Second Coming, a teaching about morality— which have nothing to do with anything that Jesus taught.

This "house of merchandise" is always arguing; it's arguing with someone else who wants to change. It wants to manipulate; it wants to become a bigger house of merchandise. It argues "about" things; whereas, the spiritual church, the church of Spirit does not allow anyone to stand in judgment of anyone, to condemn anyone, to criticize anyone. The church of Spirit always demands love — love being expressed in daily life and activity.

All the corrupt human mind points up, often expressed through the church of merchandise, is blindness to the Whole. That's all it can express—and only as you look at church as Spirit in operation, can you see the Whole. The church of merchandising can only see the part that it is merchandising. It can't see the Whole. It's impossible to see the Whole; whereas, the house of Spirit sees only Spirit and expresses Itself as selfless love-in-action.

Jesus said: "the kingdom of God"—and the kingdom of God is but another name for church —"is within you." You are church or you have no church. You have a parody on church perhaps, but you have no church.

The spiritual Church calls on us to avoid "views about" even Spirit Itself. It demands that we do more than dispute or have views about Spirit, that we actually live Spirit; because God is spirit. Every religious denomination starts with a "view about" rather than the living of Spirit. By that I mean the church will have a "view about" the nature of heaven, the Second Coming or about morality.

The moment you have a view of something you have a limited view of the Whole. It reminds me so much of a time some years ago as I was standing on the edge of a gorge and looking down into the gorge. How beautiful it seemed. But then as I stood looking into the gorge I realized that at that moment I had no view of what is termed "heaven," because my eyes were only looking down into the gorge.

It's true that looking into the gorge seemed to be beautiful and very frequently as we look out from our church of merchandise what we seem to see is sometimes beautiful, but it must be limited. By its very nature it has to be limited because it's based upon a "view about" a teaching rather than the teaching itself.

A point of view is always a point of blindness. As I said about the gorge, I had merely that point of view about looking into the gorge and I was blind to the "heavens" above. Or if I had a point of view about the "heavens" I would be limited as far as the gorge is concerned.

Churches—and it doesn't matter what church you talk about—become churches or fellowships which are blind to the greatness of the house of Spirit. They have a point of view about anything rather than a living experience (and this would apply even to Truth Center, a Universal Fellowship). Churches with a point of view, a limited view about something, accept a portion of a teaching, and calling it the whole thing, are indeed houses of merchandise. They merchandise a teaching "about" something. They may even call that a teaching about Spirit. But the house of Spirit, the spiritual Church, is and must ever remain, free from points of view about anything; free from perverse disputing of the corrupt mind.

Through the centuries the wars that mankind has engaged in have been so-called religious wars. Why? Because they were wars that expressed points of view. The moment you have points of view you have conflicts. You cannot avoid them. Then what is the solution? We must find within ourselves and then express that which we find within ourselves as selfless love expressed to others. Only as we do that are we "making not" the Father's house a house of merchandise.

Have you ever noticed how often the house of merchandise is sold as merchandise? It is sold as a theological point of view—criticizing somebody else's morals or somebody else's point of view. It merchandises a point of view. Because such churches start with a point of view they are automatically thrown into conflict with those who have a different point of view.

The house of Spirit or the church of Spirit, the kingdom of heaven, demands that we look to Spirit as the source of all activity. But in that looking, never loose contact with the needs of those around us. If we lose contact with the needs of those around us we turn our church of fellowship into nothing more than a church of fellowship of merchandise. When we refuse to see another's point of view, we turn ourself into a house of merchandise.

The spiritual church is not a teaching "about" anything. The spiritual church is that church which is found within and which encourages and demands that one live the teachings of selfless love in daily life. Your concept of church must become something much greater than the corruption of the human mind, the merchandising of a teaching "about" something.

How often individuals give money to a church and think they've given (and indeed they have given) but they have given to the church of merchandising. There is only one gift that we can give to the house of Spirit. That one gift is ourselves. Frequently ask yourself: "How much of the church of merchandising, the church of points of view 'about' something, do I entertain?" Then, having asked yourself that, remember Christ Jesus' words: "Make not my Father's house a house of merchandise."

Make your house the temple of Spirit, the temple of selfless service to God through selfless service to all of God's creation and creatures. Spirit demands such service from you. Such demands fulfilled is the only legitimate gift you can give to the church of Spirit. In short, you can only give yourself. We see individuals who come very close to this; and in thinking about it my thought went out to Albert Schweitzer, who so selflessly gave of himself. He left a career as a theologian and as probably the foremost organist in Europe of the time, to give of himself. He created of himself the church of Spirit. This led me to look up one of his quotations which I want to share with you.

"You must give some time to your fellow men. Even if it's a little thing, do something for those who have need of help, something for which you get no pay but the privilege of doing it." Notice it is "no pay." We pay for merchandise, but the demand is that we cannot accept pay. This goes right back to Jesus' statement: "Freely ye have received, freely give."

The other day I was rather interested in hearing someone say that in the 60's he "gave of himself" to a cause. He said: "But now I'm a checkbook giver. I'm still interested in all of these causes, but now I give a check." We think we give money. But if you give merely a check and that check does not come from something of yourself, you are only giving to the house of merchandise within yourself. You must give—but be careful how you give.

Make not your Father's house a house of merchandise. Rather, make it a house of Spirit through your selfless service to others.

Selfless service given to others in need, enables you to enter the Father's house and to see that that selfless service itself is the Father's house.

XXIV

GIVE FREELY

Spiritual development is an inner experience which starts with the Self.
Spiritual development is changing one's self—or
more accurately—it is being willing to be
changed by the divine Power that is the source
of one's Indentity.

The continuation of that development is a
continuation of the truth that one must reform
one's self—or be willing to let one's self be
reformed. It is not a search to find peace,
contentment, supply or anything outside of
one's Self.

Spiritual development is always in us. It
is within one's self and within the continuation
of the awareness that is within one's self
that one finds Truth. "If ye continue in my
word," Christ Jesus said, "then are ye my disciples indeed; and ye shall know the truth, and
the truth shall make you free." Continuity of

the inner experience of seeking Truth is what spiritual development is all about.

This "within-ness" is not a within-ness within one's selfish being. It is within-ness within the divine Power Itself—within what you call God or Divinity. But it must be the recognition that there is in you, within yourself, the spiritual Identity you call your Self. It is inner feeling, inner being, inner loving within one's Self that spells success as far as spiritual development is concerned.

One must be very alert that he doesn't feel that his inner experience is all there is to spiritual development. Inner feeling must lead to outer action; and unless these inner feelings lead to outer action there is no spiritual development. Then spiritual development is the process in which the inner spiritual development becomes outer spiritual action. And outer spiritual action becomes inner spiritual action.

The living within one's Self must lead to living in unity, in willingness to gather together with all of God's creation. Inner being must lead one to outer being, to outer caring; and inner loving must lead to the loving of all.

These two—the inner and the outer— must become one. The two actions—the inner action and the outer action—are actually one action. In the Gospel According to Thomas, Jesus points out that the two must become one and the one must become two. The inner must become the outer. And we must realize that

191

what we have previously thought of as the
outer is actually part of our own Self.

You cannot have inner spiritual
development separated from outer spiritual
development, nor can you have it the other
way around. You can't have all these things
you are thinking about that you've got to do
"out there," such as caring for this person and
that person, and sacrifice inner development.
The two must become one. Unless the two
become one, you are not engaging in spiritual
development. You are engaging, at best, only in
a theory about spiritual development.

Spiritual development demands action,
the inward action that becomes outward
action. In fact, your Identity must be at-one
with such action. Then spiritual development
demands a living concern and commitment for
others. There must be that living concern and
not "pocketbook concern," where you say "I
wrote a check for such and such." That might
be all right, but spiritual development demands
that one becomes a living and loving disciple,
one who is serving and not a theorist about
serving.

You must learn to free yourself from mere
dogmas about spiritual development. Every
time you think in terms of sitting down and
merely talking about Truth, or maybe even
helping somebody else to find Truth, and
feeling because you are doing some "thing" for
that person—without spiritual development
behind that "thing"—you are deceiving yourself.
It is not doing something for somebody else. It

is doing something for someone else because you have found something of your inner Being.

To spend one's time theorizing about truth and feeling that because one is thinking the truth that he is engaging in spiritual action is to deceive one's self. Because inner action, inner activity must lead to outer activity, outer action. Spiritual development does not allow you to separate the two, because they are actually one.

Spiritual development is the "process" by which we know Truth. But the Truth that we know is not a some "thing;" it's not a set of principles that you can read in a book; it's not a theory "about" God. Spiritual Truth actually is a happening. Spiritual Truth is activity. It is movement. It is the God-power in which "we live, and move, and have our being." Truth is movement. It is living. Truth is that which we live. It is that which is activity in us. It is that which is Reality in us. Truth is not a truth "about" something. Truth is the active Power Itself.

Truth is demanding of us that we live as "part" of the Whole; and Whole is but another name for God. Hence, we are called upon to live the truth, to live a communal experience, communal as part of the Whole. We are, then, residents of the community of Truth, and as such residents, we are to share—lovingly and joyously—with all the other residents of that spiritual community of Truth.

Have you ever thought that you are more than the "I." How often we go around saying "I am well; I am healthy; I am free." Psychiatrists and those in certain religions will say: "You must get a good view of yourself!" Perhaps, but something bigger is needed. You are not really an "I," you're a "we." The more you declare the "I," the more selfish you become—you can't avoid it. You are to feel not what is best for the selfish, self-centered "I," but you are to feel as the "we."

You are responsible for all of God's creation and creatures. Anyone who calls upon you is entitled to your love; but they may not call upon you in words. The whole world is calling out for peace, and they are entitled to feel you are peace—the inner that they can touch from the outer.

Truth is not a theory about something. Truth is the moving, freeing, loving reality of spiritual existence. Truth is, and that "isness" of Truth must be expressed in outward commitment and concern. For your own spiritual development, you must move beyond a mere theory about service. You must move to selfless, social service. You must see that you can find your Identity only as you recognize that you are part of the communal process of Truth.

Unless you take others in, you've left yourself out. And all the declarations that you are well, you are perfect, you are happy, will not bring you that feeling of being at-one with the source of your Being.

194

How important it is that we take time to be still, to have what can be called spiritual meditation. Unless that quiet time in spiritual meditation causes you to come out and listen to the noise of human living, it is really of no value to you. You have to take the stillness of your meditation out into the noise of the child's cry for its mother, the mother's moaning for her lost child, the battlefield's thundering torment, the sobs of the poor and homeless and the dying. Unless our quiet time enables us to hear we have but engaged in an imitation of genuine meditation.

All the noise of human living, all the tragedies of walking through this experience must be seen and faced up to as part of our individual spiritual developmnent. Without hearing the noise of human existence with its wars and rumors of wars, its poverty, its dying, spiritual development would be a fraud, would be a deception. It would be deceiving us into believing that we are advancing spiritually because we have separated ourselves for a time in quiet meditation.

Spiritual development demands that you free yourself from the fraudulent concept that stillness is all that is required, that stillness can be separated from the noise of human experience. We are called upon to live the Truth, to be the Truth, to experience the Truth. And the truth is that we are part of the Whole. The truth is that we are the stillness made manifest as love for the discomfort, pain and sorrows of others.

There must be the awareness that we are to be love-in-action to others—and especially to those we think we don't like. Jesus spends a great deal of time telling us that we have to love our enemies. If you want to advance Spiritward, learn to love your enemies. Don't try to hate them. Don't try to shoot them down. Don't try to resent them. Love them, because in that love of others—especially those we think we don't love—lies our own individual spiritual development.

The most important point of Jesus' teaching is that he expected those who had sensed his identity to do more than just glorify him as a person. Over and over he sends his disciples out. Over and over he tells them that they are to be concerned with others, to have a commitment to others. He said: "Heal the sick, cleanse the lepers, raise the dead, cast out devils." What is Jesus saying to do? Do something for others. Stop thinking first about yourself.

You may have seen those stickers at one time that people put on their desks years ago which said: "Me third. First God, then my fellow man, then me." No, not "me third." Leave yourself out of it and don't ask even that you be third. Serve others, because in the service to others you find your God—you find your own spiritual development.

What are we talking about? It is the homeless, the sick, the prisoners, those who are engaging in war. And we have several wars going on in the world right now. We've become so used to them that we probably don't know they are going on. You don't think about them day by day unless you're very much in tune with your own spiritual development. How much prayer are you giving? How much of yourself are you doing to heal these situations?

Your spiritual development demands that you do more than just silently plead God's allness. Because God's allness means including all, including every living identity. His allness demands our living of that allness, and living it as the only test of our own individual, spiritual development. Living his allness demands the concern and caring for all—and I mean all that God has created. This inner stillness must express itself as service to others in the community of Truth.

You are your brother's keeper. You are responsible to keep your brother in your own love. And unless you are willing to keep your brother in your own love, you are not advancing spiritually.

You are to "heal the sick, cleanse the lepers, raise the dead, cast out devils." Then Jesus went on to say: "Freely ye have received, freely give." That's your quiet time when you freely receive. But be sure that you are freely giving, because without that free-giving there is no spiritual growth.

"Freely ye have received." You always have that inner quietness you can go to. You don't have to wait until you can sit down and close your eyes. That inner quietness can come to you at any place, but it must express itself in action. Unless it's expressing itself in action, in freely giving, you are not taking part in your own spiritual development.

"Freely ye have received, freely give." Freely give to the whole community of Truth.

XXV

FREE-FLOWING LOVE

Love — what a wonderful word! But what is love? Do we really know what love is? We are taught from earliest childhood that we need to seek and maintain love. And most individuals usually think of love as being received and given; but if we accept that concept of love we can also withhold love.

We need a whole new view of love or maybe we need an old view of love, a love that every spiritual Teacher, including Christ Jesus, has presented to mankind from the beginning of time when there were Holy Teachers. Then what is this new-old concept of love? It is that love which flows from the inner Source, from the God within you. And love seen this way and practiced from this awareness is both continuous and inexhaustible.

How tragic it is to think that we have to "gain" love and to believe that love comes to us and goes out from us. We'll say: "We don't have to love that nation because they are not loving us; we don't have to love that group of people since they are in that position because of what they have done."

We all use that word love and now we even have postage stamps that have the word love on them. Oh, how individuals want to be loved! They want to be cared for; they want somebody to help them. In fact, I am convinced that the hunger for love is more of a human emotion than even the hunger for food.

Love becomes selfish. "I need love. Do they love me?" How often we hear someone say: "Does he love me?" Or, "Do the members of the family really love me?" We say: "Does that nation," perhaps halfway around the world, "love our nation?" All these statements indicate a concept, a misconception regarding love that is external to one's self.

There is boundless love for any individual who will but start his search for love within himself—within his true awareness of who he is as an entity at-one with the source of Love. Then boundless love is the awareness of our oneness with the divine Self. It is love that is always given. We have this boundless love and yet most individuals look out from themselves and hunger for love. And why is an individual unloved? He's unloved because he is the victim of his ignorance that love is God's activity flowing through and out from himself.

To become aware of love is a need that is common to everyone; yet most individuals seek outside of themselves for the fulfillment of this need; whereas, genuine Love can only be found within. What we most need is not more human love, but a Self-awareness that love is already within ourselves. It is this zest for awareness that is needed, awareness of the inner source of Love.

When you say you have to love yourself before you can have anybody love you—that's not true. You free yourself from that self that is wanting love so that you're not concerned whether anyone loves you or not. You are aware of your own individual, God-given oneness with the source of spiritual Love and that source is what is often called God.

How does God express His love? Through you and through me, because we are ever at-one with the great all-loving God. This God which is within you, that constantly demands that you express love, is not a God that is "out there," or a God who is a person or a thing; but you are one with the God who is love. You are not really the image and likeness of divine Love because you are actually one with Love. You are Love.

Hatred has no valid reality to the one who knows the inner source of Love. (I'm talking about negative hatred here, because there is certainly a positive hatred. You have a right to hate that which takes you away from your birthright to express love. It's your birthright to express love.)

What is hatred, this negative hatred? It is but a lie about love or the absence of love. The basic sin or evil is the belief that you can negatively hate. Not understanding the nature of love—your oneness with the Source, divine Love—you negatively hate those whom you feel do not express love or perhaps do not do what you think they should do.

God does not—and therefore you must not —negatively hate those who appear to hate Him or who appear to do evil. He does not love saints more than sinners, He just loves. Because as the Bible assures us, God is not a respecter of persons. He loves and He loves regardless of how the human mind classifies persons—whether the human mind classifies a person as good or one that is evil.

We use punishment such as capital punishment or lesser forms against individuals. Often we even hate those who do not do what we think they should do; and we hate those who see a higher way of handling this negative hatred and we are vindictive toward them. For instance, the hatred that a lot of individuals have for those who feel that there's a higher way of handling things than capital punishment.

Sometimes we even try to silence those with whom we disagree. Have you ever thought that you are not responsible for converting these people, changing these people, adjusting these people or doing anything to these people? They have to do it themselves. You are responsible only for expressing love.

No individual has ever been converted to righteous living by punishment, by vindictiveness, or by trying to silence him. But by loving we are in command of the situation. Only as we love those whom we think we hate are conversions to higher principles possible.

"An eye for an eye" is a violation of Christ Jesus' command that we are obligated to return good for evil. Living by the evil principle of "an eye for an eye" may temporarily inhibit evil deeds, but it does absolutely nothing to correct any situation.

If God is love and doesn't punish, what right do we have to punish? We sometimes let situations get out of hand; but we can't let the so-called evil person take over. Then what are we to do about such situations? We are to live our birthright and our birthright is our awareness of our oneness with the God who is love.

This God of love is not a personal God who loves an individual if that individual loves Him. God is love, and by that I mean God loves. He does not love you because you do good, nor does He hate you because you do evil. He loves because He is love. His nature is to love. He is kingdomed within you as love. Then you are only expressing your fullness when you express the love that is kingdomed within you.

Correctly understood, God does not and cannot forgive sins. Forgiveness of sins is something the human mind asks for. God, who is already loving, does not classify one as sinning and another as not sinning. God is already loving regardless of how we classify ourselves or others. It is in this sense that we can rightly say that God does not forgive sins. Actually what we think of as righteous and true forgiveness is our becoming aware of the source of divine Love within ourselves.

You can always judge a genuinely great religion; and the way you can judge it is the emphasis that is placed upon Love. All genuine religions see the importance of Love and the importance of not striking back against someone whom they think is doing evil. Individuals see the importance of not trying to do some "thing," but to let love come out from within themselves in the expressing of genuine non-resistance.

Right at this very moment you have enough spiritual Love—because you have the whole of God within you—to handle any problem.

Let Love be in you. Express Love—experience Love—and let it flow from you freely.

XXVI

GOD CONCERN

For God so loved the world, that he gave his only begotten Son, that whosoever believeth in him should not perish, but have everlasting life."

These words given in John's Gospel are words that are used quite frequently by Christians. Yet I wonder if we've really seen what a great thing is being said in this statement. Or do we reinterpret the meaning to be something less than the greatness which the writer is pointing to.

"God so loved the world." God so loved! He loved the world. He loves the world. He loves right where you are. He loves right where I am. He loves where everyone is—the world!

Then what is the nature of love? Love is selfless giving. Love is freely giving. "God so loved" that He gave. The nature of God is to always give. If God loves and God gives, what about you? If you really love—you, like God, must give.

The Gospel says that "God gave his only begotten son." God gave Jesus and what was Jesus to do? He was to do what God does—he was to give. He was to give freedom; he was to give care. Note that these are all things dealing with the worldly condition. He was to heal sickness, he was to give pardon to the sinner and comfort to the dying. He was to feed the hungry and to give love to the homeless. Jesus, like God, gave.

God not only gave Jesus to care for the world, He has given you to care for the world; He's given me to care for the world; He's given others to care for the world. He calls upon everyone to give. Divine Love, God, demands giving. We are to give our lives, give through sharing, through individual caring. Anything less, even though we talk of love, is a mockery regarding love. We have to get rid of the theory regarding love—and actually love, actually give.

One thing important to remember is that God gives to the world even though the world may not appear to be deserving of that gift. God's love is even for the undeserving. Jesus' love was for the undeserving, and you and I are called upon to give love to the undeserving as well as to those who believe that they are deserving.

The narrative doesn't say: "God so loved the world because the world was deserving of

His love." But Love gives without first checking to see whether the individual is ready for the love. Love gives and we are called by divine Love to both give love and to be love. This is perhaps one of the central themes running through the Gospel of John. Jesus taught that we are to love all and that we love whether the one to whom we are to give that love is deserving of the love or not.

If we accept Jesus literally, we are even called especially to love our enemies. The test of the love that you are to express is not that you love those who love you, but it is to love the Whole-created world; then we can't destroy the world. We are called to love the world, to take care of this world, not an imaginary, theoretical world. We're to take care of the world's environment; we're to take care of its streams and its rivers; and to take care of its land. We are to take care of the world, including everyone within it.

If Christ Jesus returned to the world today I wonder if he would be pleased with the way it's being used. Jesus wasn't talking about an abstraction called "a world hereafter." He said: "God so loved the world," this world. We are to love the whole world and everything about it.

Jesus put only one demand upon his students—that they love—and that that love be actively expressed. We are to love both the saint and the sinner, because Love is no respecter of persons. Love is that Divine quality which is ever responding to the needs of others. To remain in ignorance of the needs of others, to sometimes even persuade ourselves that others are not in need, to convince ourselves that another's problems are his problems, not ours, is to be ignorant of the great value and importance of Love.

God is concerned with the whole world. He loved and still loves the world; and we must love this world. We must use our life in this world as our schoolhouse to learn the nature of the spiritual World, the kingdom, which is "not of this world."

We spend so much time thinking about a kingdom some place else. It's this world that God loves. In fact, we will find the spiritual kingdom, symbolically stated as the kingdom of heaven, only as we love—as God loves—this world.

Spiritual development starts and ends with love expressed to this worldly experience. It is not how much you learn about love, but how much loving you do, how much caring you do for others. We spend too much time— particularly religious people—theorizing about the kingdom "not of this world," failing to realize that we find the spiritual Kingdom only as we love this world, as we protect this world, sustain this world, care for this world and everything and everyone in it.

We must become lovers of this world, because this world is an outward symbol of our love for God and of His spiritual kingdom. We can't do it the other way around. We can't do

it with a theory about a spiritual experience
that is going to come at some future time. We
start where we are living in this world. We
must love the world that "God so loved" and
loves.

If Jesus came back today I think he
would be sorely disappointed in the way in
which his name is used. He had but one
message and it is the message that is the most
needed today. That message is the message of
love, love for this world. I don't think it
would be too strong to say that the message
of love for this world demands that we protect
this world from nuclear destruction. It is the
love that you and I must express to everyone
and everything in this universe.

Previously I may have told you the story
of one of my father's cousins I was visiting.
She said she was looking forward to Jesus
coming back in the flesh; but of course Jesus
never intended that at all. He said his fleshly
experience was finished and he didn't need to
come back. In fact, he said it would be the
Spirit that would come back.

This cousin was very much interested in
that traditional sense of Christianity and she
talked frequently with me about the time when
Jesus would come back. This was at the time
when men were beginning to wear their hair
long which we would not think very much
about today, but in those days it was rather
startling. So I said to her: "Wouldn't it be nice
if Christ Jesus came next Sunday and walked
down the aisle of your church to greet you and

your pastor." And she said: "Oh, that would be just absolutely wonderful!" Then I said: "No doubt he would probably be wearing long hair." She said: "He wouldn't dare!"

Do we have a preconceived idea of what Jesus' coming means to us? The coming of Jesus to us should mean the coming of the spirit of Love that he expressed. Nothing less. He said it would be the Comforter, the Spirit, and he uses the word spirit which means without material accompaniment. Jesus was not going to come back with a material accompaniment, his body.

So often we see Jesus' name used to criticize minorities, to continue intolerance, to separate people. Sometimes we even use Jesus' name, saying: "It's for a righteous cause; because Jesus would want us to build these armaments so we can destroy the ungodly."

Did Jesus say that God so loved the world that He sent him — or at other times other individuals — to take care of only the saints, or was his message to love everyone? We are called to love; we are called to love the world and those who are in it who need that love. We are to give our love to the poor, to the homeless, to the hungry, to the disenfranchised. Let us learn that we are to love all, everyone, everywhere. Let it be said of us that we so love; that we, like God, give ourselves selflessly and universally.

210

As you know, I am very fond of the Phillips translation of the New Testament. I'd like to read the words that Jesus gave to Nicodemus that night so many centuries ago. "For God loved the world so much that he gave his only Son so that everyone who believes in him should not be lost, but should have eternal life." I wonder what Nicodemus thought when Jesus said this, among other things that he told him.

Have you ever thought that each of you are an only son and that the Father's love is going to you at that very moment? If you want to get a good illustration of that, go to the story of the Compassionate Father, or as it's sometimes called, the Prodigal Son. The father had only two sons and he said: "All that I have" belonged to each of them. Either one could have had all that he had.

Actually the literal meaning of this statement in the Greek is unique, one who is like no other. This brings us to the question of individuality, that each one of you is created uniquely. God loves you uniquely. You are unique; you are an only son. (Today maybe we should also say an only daughter.) Jesus was a unique individual. It was this uniqueness of Jesus that enabled him to find eternal Life. You are like Jesus—unique. And in that uniqueness—in that individuality—is eternal Life for you.

What does it mean to believe in him? To do what he did. You believe in someone only when you do what they do. It doesn't mean believe in his name, but to do what he did. To believe in him is to believe in his message and life — and do as he did. He did it in a unique way; and you are also called upon to live your life in a unique way.

Jesus never considered himself a personal Savior. And no blind belief in Jesus or any other Holy individual—even in the belief that Jesus is a personal Savior—can give you eternal Life. There is only one way to find eternal Life and that is to express your unique ability to love.

On one occasion "there came one running...and asked him, "Good Master, what shall I do that I may inherit eternal life?" Did Jesus say to accept him as a good, personal Savior? That's what traditional Christianity too often says. Just accept me as a personal Savior and I will give you eternal Life. But Jesus' answer was: "Why callest thou me good? there is none good but one, that is, God." This is a complete denial on Jesus' part that he was a personal Savior. You find goodness only when you find God in yourself. It's as if Jesus were saying: "Don't come to me as a personal Savior; if you do, you're going to get lost. Don't call me good. I'm not a personal Savior, because you have to save yourself."

Then he gave an answer to the man. What were these things he was to do? "Thou knowest the commandments, Do not commit adultery, Do not kill, Do not steal, Do not bear false witness, Defraud not, Honour thy father and mother."

The man said: "All these things have I kept from my youth up." He was a religious man, he'd done these things. "Now when Jesus heard these things, he said unto him, Yet lackest thou one thing." And this is so apparent today. You can talk about love, theorize about love, and even go around hugging everybody that comes in sight; but it is doing, it is caring for this world and those that are therein.

Then Jesus said: "Sell all that thou hast and distribute unto the poor." In short, love. He saw that this man had a theory. I'm not sure that he meant for this man to literally sell everything, but to sell his concept, because he had a theoretical concept about the commandments. What he was to do was to do something about the poor.

All this theorizing about a personal Savior will never accomplish anything. In fact, it can be a negative force because it enables one to feel that as long as he is a new-born individual then he doesn't have to think about his being saved hereafter. There is only one way to be saved hereafter and that is to be saved here. Let the "after" take care of itself.

We need to ask ourselves: What have I done this past week about the poor? What are we going to do next week? Jesus' words were to "Sell all that thou hast and distribute unto the poor." In short, take care of this world, love this world, those that are in this world. And then—and then only—"thou shalt have treasure in heaven." Then you are able to follow him; that's the only Savior there is, following what he said to do.

Let it be said of you and of me, that we so love this world that we give to the world and to everything and everyone therein.

XXVII

THE FLOWER AND THE HONEYBEE

In the gospels, on one occasion, Christ Jesus said: "The kingdom of God is within you." The kingdom is where God resides —within you.

God is that divine Power that you express when you are willing to realize that there is, beyond the experience that you have thus far lived, a Power. It's what Jesus referred to when he said: "My kingdom is not of this world."

There are two concepts of power. There is the power of this world where it becomes the power that money gives or the power that is expressed by a powerful nation. But there is another Power, the Power of one's own spiritual life. The greatest Power in the world is the spiritual life that gathers together with the small group ("two or three gathered together") in which no sense of personal gain is sought.

The Power is not something that you are reaching "out there" for; nor is it something that you have to learn about, go through a series of talks or attend church services in an attempt to define God—or even to find Him. It is not talking "about" Truth, but it is a living Force that we are called upon to express.

People want to argue about Truth, but Truth isn't something that you argue about. In fact, I've often said to individuals who are defining God: "I think that God should be defined as a verb rather than a noun," because it is not God as a "thing," but it is God as a power within.

It would be very easy to say: "Don't you have a teaching about that?" No, my calling is for the living of this Truth rather than the talking about Truth. Then the question follows: "How do you do this?" It's summarized very clearly in a statement by Jesus. You may recall that he had been talking about those who wanted to gain things, material possessions and health; and Jesus said: "Seek ye first the kingdom of God, and his righteousness; and all these things" that he had been talking about "shall be added unto you" in a new light, with a new force of importance to you. We are so prone to think that we are to judge spirituality by the things that we gain, the things we possess; but it is quite the reverse. It is seeking first.

Have you ever known anyone who always does something first and then says: "Come on, God, help me out!" He wants to rush to do

216

this, do that, do the other thing, instead of sitting down and finding within himself the spiritual kingdom. He wants to find out why this isn't working out some way, why that isn't working out and always trying to "do" something. There are those who go to the other extreme. They sit back and say: "When the Spirit moves me I'll move." It is seeking first the kingdom of God, that God-power within yourself that is actively expressing Himself through you and as you.

You may say: "Is it as simple as that?" Yes, it is, but it requires a sacrifice in order to do it. You must give up something for it. If you study the gospels you are going to find that Jesus demanded of those who came to him a giving up of something. It is the willingness to give up that is required; and those who were unable to do so were not accepted as his followers.

Perhaps you are acquainted with the story of the woman who came and touched Jesus' garment. Virtue went out from him, healing went out from him, help went out from him. Unlike the usual teaching of today, I contend that it is not trying to heal people, but becoming so spiritually aware of one's own Identity that other people can touch you.

But you say: "What do you mean by this 'touching'?" Perhaps this "touching" could best be explained by the honeybee. The honeybee touches a flower, but a flower doesn't say: "I have to change the honeybee; I have to make a new honeybee; I've got to do something to that honeybee; I've got to manipulate that honeybee." The flower merely lets the honeybee touch it; and all spiritual healing is that touching experience.

It is becoming the flower so that the honeybee can touch. It is finding your spiritual identity so that those who want to come to you can come and be helped and blessed. The wonderful part is that others do not have to be in personal contact with you. People can reach out to you from no matter where and feel the influence, the power, the support, the guidance that comes from this spirituality. Being the "flower" is the spiritual Reality of your own existence coming into play.

The interesting thing is that the person who is the "flower," the person who has found his spiritual Identity, is not concerned with the changes that take place "out there." Those looking on will see the changes; but he does not spend his time saying: "I was so spiritual today that I healed someone, I changed so-and-so or somebody was blessed by coming in contact with me." The moment he does that he is admitting that he is a person doing these things.

There is, in spiritual development, no manipulation—no trying to use one's human mind to change or manipulate somebody, to drag someone else into the kingdom of heaven. You are responsible for no one but yourself. You are responsible for keeping yourself so spiritually attuned that you can be touched and become the reformation for the whole world.

We are obligated to be so uplifted that, like Christ Jesus, we can be touched—and virtue, that is, our own spiritual development—can go out to bless, to heal and to redeem. We must become the modern disciples who go into all the world to heal the sick.

Prayer in its highest sense includes everyone in it. Actually, there can be no such thing as selfish prayer. It is always prayer for others. It is always the prayer in which you have gained so spiritually that others can reach you and feel your oneness with this great Power.

When you find this Other Worldliness, those around you feel the influence of what you are. But I do not want to leave you with the impression that this has no practical effect in the human experience. It is this Other Worldliness lived that is the only valid Force.

You are all acquainted, I'm sure, with that statement of Jesus where he said: "Heal the sick, cleanse the lepers, raise the dead, cast out devils." Most people stop there, but the rest of the statement is "Freely ye have received, freely give."

XXVIII

NO OTHER CHOICE

We say that God is the supreme Being —the infinite Being—or that God is infinite personality, but God is not really a being at all. He is not a person or a thing; nor is He a God who adjusts or creates to suit His personal pleasure at some particular time.

God is the All in All. He is in every created, living thing. He is not some thing or some one. He is spirit, the great I AM. He is the God that Moses recognized as the I AM THAT I AM. And God can only be worshiped when we see Him as he truthfully is, as Spirit.

God is not a power that you go to, to adjust human situations. He is the Source, the source of all existence. He is the source of all reality—He is—and you cannot go beyond that. You must worship Him that way—you haven't any choice. Any other worship is not worship at all.

Christ Jesus gave an entirely different view of God from the God of his time. It was thought that God was "out there" some place, that one went to the Father. But he said quite simply that "God is spirit." Jesus came to free us from the sense that God is a Father separated from us; and we find our freedom best when we separate ourselves from the sense of God as being a person "out there" some place. To Jesus, God was a spiritual Father within one's self which one could go to at any time.

What was Jesus saying when he said "God is spirit"? The very word spirit means without material accompaniment, without material parts or personality. This doesn't mean that you lose your concept of God by getting a revitalized, renewed, redemptive sense of God. It gives you the only God there is. It gives you the God that is "isness," the "isness" underlying all reality.

To argue about God and His nature or which church expresses God the most, accomplishes nothing. The great need today is for the return of Christianity to Jesus and his concept of God—the God of spirit—the God of love. You must have a a true concept of what your God is; and you must recognize that since He is spirit, you can reach Him only as you yourself recognize that He is the fathering Force of spirit within yourself.

Christ Jesus said it so plainly when he said: "They that worship him must worship him in spirit and in truth." And notice it is "must."

221

You must worship Him that way, you haven't any other choice. Any other worship is not worship at all. The worship which gets down into moral issues, money raising and trying to change things, these things that Christianity so often engages in, is not a tribute to the one God in any way—at least not to Jesus' God.

Much of what is thought of today as worship is quite foreign to spirituality and to truthfulness. Only when we recognize God to be what He is, spirit, are we enabled to go directly to Him, and going directly to Him within one's self is the only genuine worship there is.

You need no intermediaries between you and your God. You have no church between you and your God. You can have no priesthood between you and your God, no so-called "spiritual practitioner" between you and your God. There can be no personal savior standing between you and your God. You are at-one with your God now and your God is spirit, infinite Spirit.

This God of spirit is the source of what John saw so clearly when he said: "God is love." God is the source of love; He is the source within you which recognizes that you must see every other individual as created equal with yourself. We say "God is love" and of course love is one of the characteristics of God; but God is more than just love as a characteristic, because actually there are no characteristics to God. God is Himself love.

Love means giving. "God so loved" that He gave. God is that giving Force within you. Spiritually understood you are one with God. God is that spiritual source within you which prompts you to give, to place the Whole ahead of your own personal likes or dislikes. To fail to give God's love freely to another is to appear to withhold God's love from yourself. Give freely, without any desire whatsoever to receive for your giving.

You are created to give, to be love-in-action. Since you are one with the God that "so loved the world," you yourself must so love the world. You must give to the world and to everyone and everything within the world. And you must give freely.

You need to ask yourself: Is my concept of God a concept that is prompted by giving? Or do I sometimes even become the one who not so loves the world, but even gets down to hating part of the world? "I hate most of those people in that country."

You misuse your concept of God whenever you use Him to get something selfishly for yourself. That's not why you go to God. You go to God so that you can give; and you go to Him leaving your care in the hands of Him who "so loved." You don't go to Him to try to manipulate Him into giving to you.

Rushing around smartly doing a lot of humanly good deeds is not what I mean; although humanly good deeds will undoubtedly follow and be the by-product. But it is giving

223

out of your awareness that the God who so loves has already given to you. Jesus said it so well when he said: "Freely ye have received." Where did you receive it from? From God—and from Holy Teachers. In Jesus' case he was talking to his disciples who had undoubtedly freely received from him. But they also received from him an awareness of God.

Why is it important that Jesus should make such a statement? Because it is only through you, through me and through others that God does his giving. He needs us as givers. You are ever at-one with Him—hence you must give. You have no choice to say: "I'll give if it works out fine for me to give, but not if it's not convenient for me to give." You have no choice whether you give or you do not give— you must give; you must love.

The only proof of your understanding of God and your spiritual relationship to Him is to be found in your willingness to sacrifice, to give, and to give selflessly. And why must you selflessly give? Simply because God is always selflessly giving to you.

Someone once came to Jesus and asked to be shown the Father, the Father that loves, and Jesus replied: "He that hath seen me hath seen the Father." Why could the Master so answer? Simply because he was aware of his oneness with his Father, the fathering Force of selfless love.

Jesus was aware that he was one with the God of spirit. And the result of this awareness was his giving, the giving of himself selflessly. The by-product of this awareness was that the sick were healed, the so-called sinner was saved, the fatherless were comforted, the hungry fed and the homeless were sheltered.

What would happen if someone sincerely asked you the same question that was asked of Jesus so many centuries ago? If someone asked you to show them your God, what would you do? Would you start telling them that God lives in heaven? Would you say you've got to find a personal savior to reach Him or that you have to go to such and such a church? Would you do any of those things? Or could you, like Jesus, point to your spiritual Self and know that since you are one with your God who is spirit and love, you are in a very real and spiritual sense, God-in-action.

Out of your spiritual Awareness of your oneness with the God that so gives, the sick must be healed, the so-called sinner saved, the fatherless comforted, the hungry fed and the homeless sheltered. Unless that is happening, you do not understand your God. Unless this by-product of what you think you know of God —unless it is experienced—you have only an impractical theory about your God and your relationship to Him.

Are you aware that this God of spirit so loves and that the only test of your spiritual development, your spirituality, is that you recognize that you are His representative; and that therefore, you too must "so love"? The Law still stands that if you have freely received from the creative Source who is love, you must give—you must freely give. You have no justification in doing anything else.

Do you actively realize that you are God's chosen vessel for God? Spiritually understood, you are God-in-action. Then you are a giver of God's love—to pour out His love, to give to the world that He so loves.

Like God Himself, you are to so love the world that you give. For it is in giving that you feel your oneness with Him who is giving love.

XXIX

THE GOD OF CHAOS AND ORDER

Sometimes organized Christianity, as its primary purpose, seems to be engaged in selling real estate—real estate in heaven. It preaches that we are to find heaven as our permanent home, but this is not even in accord with the teachings of the founder of Christianity, Christ Jesus.

Organized Christianity continues all too frequently to preach that heaven is a place; but spiritually understood, heaven is not a place at all. Jesus said plainly that heaven was not a place. It was not "lo here! or, lo there!" but that "the kingdom of God is within you."

Organized religion says that heaven is a place where all is order, where one can loll about as if floating on a cloud, as it is sometimes portrayed, in perfect order, perfect harmony. Frankly, I cannot think of any place that would be duller than a place with no activity. Certainly heaven is all order and spiritually understood we must accept heaven to be the inner Realm of all order, everything in its place. But spiritually understood heaven is also divine chaos. I did not say chaos, but divine chaos; nor do I say that heaven is all order. It is divine Order.

The words chaos and order are not used here as they are generally known. I am using them to indicate divine activity, an activity that is within each individual if he but has spiritual eyes to see.

We need to see that God, being all, is in chaos and in order. He is the All in all. He is all order and He is in all chaos. He is not separate from chaos nor, correctly perceived, is chaos in competition with order. In fact, chaos and order compliment each other.

To the Western mind the word chaos usually indicates disorder, a mess, confusion—something bad which must be changed or at least improved upon. Sometimes we even think that chaos is the evidence that one is in some way displeasing God and therefore, God is giving him chaos. But we need to find a new and more spiritual view of chaos. We should use chaos, not as something which if changed will bring about order, but to see divine Order right in the midst of chaos.

The Prophet Isaiah quotes God as saying: "Behold, I create new heavens and a new earth: and the former shall not be remembered, nor come into mind." God is the

228

new heaven and new earth—the heaven of order and the earth of chaos. He is ever creating in you His new heaven and His new earth, His new order and new chaos.

God forgets Himself in you so that you can remember Him in action. This forgetting of God in you is the only real heaven to be obtained. God forgets Himself in you as order within you. But God also forgets Himself in you as chaos within you. God has gone forth and buried Himself in you as His chosen vessel to be spiritual and material action.

We see chaos and we want to bring order out of chaos. It is right that order should have its influence upon chaos; but we should not swing over and try to make frustrated and unnecessary changes in chaos.

We are in perpetual movement, ever active movement. This active movement leads us to move into chaos and at other times towards order. It is in movement, and not primarily in states of static meditation, that all spiritual birth takes place. And this birth always includes chaos and order.

These two, chaos and order, are the Ying and the Yang. Do you know where the expression of the Ying and the Yang originated? They refer to the two sides of a hill. The Ying was the shady side and the Yang was the sunny side. Hence, by extension, we think of the Ying as the shadowy part of life—darkness, chaos, unhappiness or coldness and think of the Yang as light, order, happiness and warmth.

All spiritual growth takes place by the action of chaos (the Ying) acting on the order (the Yang); and the order (the Yang) acting on chaos (the Ying). There is no spiritual order, no Yang, without chaos, the Ying. In order to understand that we have to know that good and bad, right and wrong, order and chaos, used as absolutes by Western minds and expressed in the thought of organized Jewish and Christian religions, play no part in genuine spiritual growth.

Genuine spiritual growth (and genuine spiritual growth is genuine creation) is not a creation in time. Genuine growth takes place when balance is maintained by the individual between chaos and order of his existence. Spiritual growth appears to be hampered when we become unbalanced, when we swing unnecessarily towards chaos or swing unnecessarily too far towards order.

In order for you to advance spiritually, to have spiritual births and rebirths—spiritual creation—you will need to free yourself completely from your previously held concepts of chaos and order, bad and good, right and wrong as God-given absolutes. You will also have to free yourself from the idea of a God in an ancient past as a creative being. In fact, you will have to free yourself from your concept of God as a person—either one person, three persons in one, or many persons in one.

All dogmatic theology or theories about God have to be laid aside if you are to take part in the creation of the new heaven and the new earth within yourself. I did not say that God must be laid aside, but that we need to put aside all theories about God.

God is not "out there" some place. He is, as Christ Jesus and other Holy Men have declared Him to be, holy, totally complete as Spirit. And where is this God of spirit housed? He is housed or kingdomed within all. He is kingdomed within you as spiritual chaos and spiritual order. In fact, He is the chaos and order of your being.

Avoid all thought that Spirit, God, is only to be found in the sunshine experiences of your life; or that you can only go to Him when you have difficulty in the chaos experiences of your life. Difficulties — and I would say all difficulties in life—arise out of our desire to swing between the two extremes of order and disorder. And that's an unwise desire.

All spiritual growth, all spiritual creation, all spiritual birth is accomplished through the keeping of this chaos and order in balance. Whether we are aware of it or not, all of life is the search for this balance.

You will feel His presence most when you find that it is not your personal self which brings about the balance between the chaos and order of your life. It will not be your human will, your human determination to keep chaos and order in balance; but it is He that is within you which is keeping you in balance.

You will feel Spirit's presence most when you realize the chaos of your being must be balanced by order; and the order of your being must be balanced by chaos. When you realize this, you know that you are taking part in the new creation, the birth and rebirth which you are experiencing as the new heaven and the new earth.

As you spiritually perceive your spiritual and complete individuality you will see that you are a balance between latent order and latent chaos.

XXX

GOD IS MORE THAN ATTRIBUTES

Religious thinkers like to talk about the attributes of God, such as love and peace. They say God expresses Himself through love or through peace, or God expresses Himself through health.

Perhaps for teaching purposes we need to refer to God's attributes; but we need to become aware that God does not really have any attributes at all. He is Himself His own attributes. For instance, He does not express love as an attribute of His nature. He is Himself, Love.

When I say Himself, one should not be thinking of a person. Jesus defined Him as: "God is Spirit: and they that worship him must worship him in spirit and in truth." As Christ Jesus and other religious leaders throughout time have pointed out, God is spirit. Only spirit is omnipresent. Matter appears to come into being for a time and then to disappear.

233

But Spirit and only Spirit is that which is ever-present.

We spend too much time talking and thinking about the presence of God's attributes. What is important is not the fleeting presence of His attributes, expressed as love, peace or health, but the primary and everpresence of the attributes themselves, of God Himself.

In the past, what we have perhaps thought of as attributes of God, is in reality, God Himself. It is not God expressing the attribute of Love, but that God is love; God is spirit. He does not express Himself as the attribute of peace, He is peace.

God is actually more—yes, infintely more —than an attribute called spirit, love or peace. He is Himself, spirit, love or peace. The moment we attempt to break down our concept of God into the attributes we believe He represents—at that moment we lose our clear concept and our nearness to God. (Or at least we appear to do so.)

God is spiritual Reality without need of or even the ability to express any attribute. He is the attribute. He is more than a being expressing attributes, He is all. He is all-power, omnipotent. As you think about this, it will change your view of God and your ability to find your own spiritual nature.

This omnipotence, this Power is omnipresent. It is present for you to express in its wholeness, not in a certain number of attributes which you may express at any one time. God's omnipotence is His omnipresence and His omnipresence is His omnipotence. His great power is what we could call omnipotent.

God is omni-reality, all reality, the reality of Spirit; and there is a genuine relationship between this reality of Spirit and all living identities. God does not act upon and endeavor to change individuals; He would see no need for such a change. He is omnipresent Reality, ever being at-one with all living beings and that being includes you.

God is at-one with you and you are at-one with God. Jesus recognized for himself this interconnection between God and himself when he said: "I and my Father are one." You too should accept this for yourself and say: "I and the fathering spirit of Reality are one right now," this fathering Spirit expressing Itself as you. You are at-one with the omnipresence of God; you are at-one with the omnipotence of God; you are at-one with the omni-reality of God.

You must awaken yourself to realize that you must do more than think of God as the all powerful God to whom you must appeal for His blessing. To do so would be to think of God much as a child thinks of a human father to whom he must plead for some good. Such a human father may or may not bestow good upon his offspring for the pleading. He may be a loving father or a hard father. He may give, he may withhold. But God is not such a father, loving one time and hating at another. He is

235

not a Presence acting upon or manipulating another. He is the Presence ever at-one with all living reality; and this Presence, this God, cannot be comprehended through pleading to a being "out there" some place.

God is not a father being a father; in fact He is not a being. He is being His own Reality and in that sense He is being. But He is not being as we usually think of that word being. He is Himself—Reality. He is spirit. He is. He is the I AM THAT I AM.

God is not the supreme being, if by that word being we mean a person or a thing. And of course to be a person or a thing would be to defy Christ Jesus' definition of God as Spirit. God is Himself spiritually supreme. He is not a person or being expressing supremacy, He is Himself supreme Reality. So we are faced with a paradox, because God is not a being who is ever-present being Himself; He is not a being, being Spirit expressing the attribute of Spirit. He is not a being expressing love—expressing the attribute of Love. He is not a being, bringing about or expressing peace. He is being His own supremacy here and now. He is being spirit because He is spirit. He is being love because He is love. He is being peace because He is peace.

To wait for a future time in the Christian philosophy would be to wait for a heaven. It would be a time in the human scheme of things when we would think of God as being supreme and to have a misunderstanding regarding the very nature of God. To be aware of God as divine Spirit, as divine Reality, as omni-reality is to free oneself from the attributes which ignorance makes us attribute to Him.

We accept certain limitations and then we become the victim of those limitations. We have only so much money; we have only so much health; we have only so much time—and then we become the victims. Have you ever been tempted at times to say: "I have so much to do I can't get this done, I can't get that done!"

Being aware of your oneness with the "isness" of God (not being aware of your oneness with some of the attributes of God) you can do the impossible. You can do the impossible not because you are violating either the laws of nature or the laws of God, but because you are God's law in action.

We need to realize that we are at-one with the God that can do all things—even things which humanity believes to be impossible. But those things are not things that are the manipulation of the human scene. The things that Spirit does are in the spiritual Realm and the by-product is what we may at times call a miracle. We need to keep in mind that there is no need for God to overrule the so-called laws of nature, or to overrule the inhumanity of man to man. He is, and none of these laws of nature nor the inhumanity of man plays a part in this in any way—except as a by-product.

God is and His "isness" is expressing Itself through you right now. Being aware of this, you can do the impossible—or which the human mind says is impossible. In fact if I were to define the kingdom of God I would say that the kingdom of God is the Realm of the fulfillment of the impossible.

We do not seek to make miracles happen, there's no need for us to do that; we let God do what He is, not as a being, but what He is as omnipresent Reality. We don't look far-off for a miracle, not even the miracle of a heaven hereafter.

We almost turn even the word miracles into an attribute for God. So often we say: "God expresses Himself through miracles." But being one with God who is Himself the miracle, we are ourselves the miracle. And being the miracle, we no longer look as they say the Christians do, for a man called Jesus to return to earth to establish the kingdom of heaven on earth. We don't need to wait for that, because that is a present reality, a present possibility.

"As in heaven, so on earth." The miracle of God expressing Himself right here and now need not wait until some event would take place, such as Jesus coming and returning to earth; because what would that mean? It would mean that we would have to wait for God to express His power until some human event took place such as a man called Jesus coming back into this experience. God is present now. Then what has happened to all the people in the meantime? The kingdom of

238

heaven is the miracle within yourself. It is not a miracle of a man returning to establish a kingdom on earth.

Knowing our oneness with God, we are aware that unless we are the kingdom of God within ourselves—that is, unless God is living, kingdomed within us—the kingdom of God will never come, not even with the coming of a Holy Man called Jesus. But the kingdom has come to you now. And it has come in the way that the Founder of Christianty said it had to come when he said "the kingdom of God is within you."

In one sense you create the kingdom of heaven. You do it here and now—and not at some future time—when you live as God's messenger of love and peace. Correctly and spiritually understood, you already have the kingdom of God on earth—nay—more than that, you are the kingdom of God on earth. You are already heaven kingdomed within your Self. Recognizing your oneness with your divine Parent is being in the kingdom of God.

Leave the misconception that your spiritual growth will express more fully the attributes of God. Viewed correctly, you are doing more than expressing the attributes of God, you are one with God and you are one with Him right now and forever. You are being God's holy messenger; you are being God-in-action.

All you need to do is to do more than try to be the attributes of God; and recognize for

yourself your eternal oneness with the
fathering Power.

XXXI

SILENCE IS FORGETTING

We think of worship as the outward symbols and forms of worship, but actually we worship through silence. Active silence is feeling Divinity's presence and this active silence is genuine worship. It is actually feeling the presence of Divinity within one's own experience.

We are actively silent only when we are experiencing selflessness. Or, to word it differently, this active silence is the silence of communion with the Source of your divine Self. Then active silence is actually Divinity's presence experienced. And Divinity's presence has to be experienced. Anything less is not genuine meditation or active silence.

You cannot have Divinity through a teaching about Divinity or through a theorizing about Divinity. It can only be gained through the active feeling of Divinity's presence. And where do you feel this Divinity?

241

You feel it in active silence. Silence is something that is with you everywhere, because Spirit is omnipresent.

In one of Christ Jesus' remarks he said: "God is spirit." Divinity is spirit—the only thing that is everywhere present; no matter where you go or what you do, Spirit is there. Wherever you are you have the privilege and the duty to express the active silence and God's divine presence is felt only in active silence. The most intimate contact you will have with your God is in silence—silent worship.

Silence is the active period of forgetting about your own self, your own self-centeredness, your personal wants, your personal likes and dislikes. You cannot enter the silence; you cannot worship Divinity unless you are willing to silence the self-centered self.

Do you think of yourself as merely a mortal who takes time to be apart from worldly activity? That is not active silence. Active silence is when you forget about yourself, forget about whether you are hearing God's presence or not. This seems like a paradox because we don't often think of forgetfulness as an active quality.

When I say active silence, be sure that you are not still holding on to the concept that you go off into a corner and close your eyes and put your hands on your forehead or bow the head. This may be a good way to start, but your active silence is that which is going on all the time. You may be talking to your best friend, but underneath you are expressing your active silence. You may be talking to your worst enemy; underneath you are expressing active silence.

The period we call active silence is the period in which you forget yourself, your personal self with its "I want, I think, I love" or perhaps "I hate." You enter the active silence to find and live your divine Self as opposed to your self-centered self. And you can only enter this silence through spiritual forgetfulness. Sometimes this seems to be a rather difficult task; and to the one who is steeped in himself, it can appear to be a very difficult experience. But sooner or later — and hopefully sooner — entering this silence must be done. It is the silence of selflessness. It is the silence of communion with the divine Source of your divine Self.

Who does God choose as His chosen vessel for His goodness to be poured? It is the one who has left behind his self-centered, personal self. Such a one Divinity uses to bestow His love, yes, to bestow his goodness on all His creation and creatures. You can be one of those chosen vessels if you are willing to enter the Realm of active silence.

You need not spend your time going from one religious teacher to another, going from one religious practitioner to another or from one church to another in order to find the God who is already the source of your active, silent worship. Because if you have already found your Oneness you will be living your Oneness.

One who has found his Oneness can be a tremendous help to you in your advance Spiritward. That one may be a Teacher or a particular teaching; but you must keep in mind that eventually you have to leave behind Teacher and teaching and find your own individual link with your God. If we are not alert we will still hold on to a Teacher and a teaching. But you have no intermediator. You can have no person between you and your God. A genuine Teacher can only point the way.

How do you find this link between you and your God? By being selfless and by being selfless I mean living your divine Self. It is in living your divine Self that you find your God. And where do you find Him? Not in an abstraction of stillness where you sit down and think abstractly about God. You find Him in everything and in everyone. You find Him through selfless service to everything and everyone, for you and all of God's creatures and creation are but one.

You will never be able to find Him by worshiping in static meditation or in self-centered prayer, the prayer that is always praying for yourself. You will only find your link with Divinity through the giving of your divine Self in divine service. By divine service I mean selfless service—giving to the poor, the sick, the drug addict, the homeless and those in need. In order to do this you will need to let the childlikeness in you be free.

It will not be the adult in you that has learned all these formal things that will be able to establish your link with your God. Only the child in you is able to be your freedom from the sin of value-judging another. And value-judging of others is one of the things which keep you from being your Self.

The moment you make a value judgment, whether that value judgment is good or evil makes no difference. You do not engage in value judgments of others. You don't pass judgments on whether that person is doing the right thing or the wrong thing. You must find the importance of freeing the child in you. A child doesn't pass judgment and the child in you must be free so that you do not do it. You make no value judgments about anyone else or tell other people what is good or bad for them.

Be sure that you don't have in your service to others a little sense of "this gives me a great deal of joy to do this," that nice personal sense of joy. You do it because it's the thing to do for your own spiritual development—not because it brings you joy or pain. You don't have absolutes about whether this is good for you to do or bad for you to do.

Your worship must be free from all requests for what you want. There is only one valid request. You can word it in many different ways, but the one valid request is for spiritual Light, illumination. Ask yourself why you exist in this experience. You exist for but one reason and that reason is that you have the spiritual enlightenment to experience your oneness with your God. And how do you do this? By working out your relationship through the sacrifice of the willful self so that your divine Self may selflessly serve others. No one has ever worked out his divine destiny who has not found himself as God's vessel out of which God pours His goodness on the world.

You don't have to enter the silence in order to have God speaking to you. God is speaking to you, but you hear him best when you are worshiping Him through service to others. This service must ever remain silent. When I am talking about silence, that silence is —or at least ought to be—expressed in the midst of the noise and pressures of this world. Don't try to separate yourself from the cares of this world in order to find and to experience the silence. You must be in the world doing the things of the world in order to experience active silence; and this active silence is spiritual worship.

No one who is engaging in selfless service is talking about or bragging about or even finding personal comfort in the service that he is bestowing. To talk about, brag about, find comfort in personal service is to admit — whether one realizes it or not—that one is not engaging in genuine service. In short, the service that we have to engage in is so pure, so self-effacing that not even the right hand knows what the left hand is doing.

Only the one who has a heart big enough to be of service is a saint. How often we use the word saint so glibly. "He is a real saint!" Watch that you make a distinction between service and selfless service. There are a lot of people doing a lot of things. They say: "He takes such good care of his wife" or his brother or his mother, or whoever it happens to be. I am not talking about that kind of service. It is service that comes right out of the heart. I'm talking about a service that is making a home in one's heart for all, especially the downtrodden.

We should be so engaged in spiritual service that we have no time to think about our personal self with its problems and willfulness. I don't mean by that that your personal problems won't be taken care of, but they should merely be a by-product of your own willingness to serve.

You enter the silence to find spiritual enlightenment. In the silence you become aware that as God's chosen, you, like your God are light. In the darkness there is Light and you are the chosen vessel to bring that Light to this world. But you can only be that chosen vessel in the ratio that you are willing to let your self-centered self vanish.

God is the light and you are called by Divinity to be the light to those in the darkness of the shadows of want, of disease, of unhappiness. Let the Light—that is, let God— permeate you. And the Light permeates you as service in which you see God revealing Himself to you.

To see this Light and to be this Light of service is to see God. But to see the Light is not really to see God, it is to be God; it is to be God-in-action. It is to be the God of spirit. It is to be, in a very real sense, the God of selfless service.

In a very spiritual sense, you are the ray of God. Actually, you're more than just a ray of God, you are yourself the Light of the world.

XXXII

ENTER THE RIVER JORDAN

Repentance has long been associated with a theological teaching; but we sometimes fail to realize that repentance is among the most important teachings if one is to find spiritual development. Yet how little repentance is taught and preached today. And if it is taught and preached, it is ignorantly presented in a way quite different than the repentance which Christ Jesus taught.

Certainly one of the great messages of the Bible is the teaching regarding repentance. The Old Testament is full of stories about repentance. What does it mean in the Old Testament when it says "a king repents"? It means that the king surrendered to the will of God and then he acted upon that repentance. Character after character in the Old Testament surrendered to God and in that surrender, in that repentance, found their way to a greater service to God and their fellow man.

In the New Testament there's even a clearer call to its readers for repentance. The simple straightforward message of John the Baptist was repentance. He came out of the wilderness to the River Jordan and said: "Repent ye: for the kingdom of heaven is at hand."

According to Mark's gospel, the words "repent" and "believe the gospel" (the good news) were among the very first words of Christ Jesus' preaching. He undoubtedly knew that repentance and the acceptance of the holy message were interconnected. One could not be attained without the other. Among Jesus' last utterances were the instructions to his disciples that the repentance and forgiveness of sins were to be preached in his name to all nations.

Repentance needs to be understood in the light of what Christ Jesus and other Holy Men have demanded of themselves and of the students that they had around them. This is true from the earliest times. We need to think what the word repentance means. Perhaps we get a clearer view of the word when we realize what its root meaning is.

The word comes from the Greek and in original Greek the two words which make up our word repentance meant "change" and "mind." Literally, repentance is a change of mind. It is a "new view." It is the tremendous change of mind, heart and life which is brought about in an individual, not by human willfulness wanting to change, not by his deciding that he wants to repent; but repentance is brought about through hearing the voice of God and obeying the dictates of the heart. Repentance is that change which is produced on an individual by Divinity Itself, by responding to the power of God within himself.

Genuine repentance is much more than a mere human desire to do better, to live better, to be better. Repentance is much more, infinitely more, than just the desire to be good, as laudable as such a desire may be. It is much more than a change of mind. It is the change of life itself. It is the transformation of life. It is a transformation of one's plans, emotions, ethics, values and actions.

This change called repentance is brought about by the power of God, by the discovery of and the living of the divine Power within one's self. It is not something that one can do by mere human will. It is not something where one can "will himself" to repent. Such a desire can often later change to a desire to be less, to do less, to live less than one is capable as a spiritual idea of God. Then repentance is that spiritual working of God in an individual and it is brought about by the action of the God-power upon individuals and groups of individuals.

Reformation gives us the ability to view the world through God's eyes instead of through our own eyes. In short, repentance is surrender to God's will, the surrender that brings about transformation. Repentance is surrender to the will of God for an individual, surrender of the self-centered and egotistical self—the self that says: "I know what is best" and has to work it out his way. It is a complete surrender. It is the surrender of the self-centered self to the spiritual Self, to the Self which God is ever revealing Himself to every individual.

Repentance is a determination that we will not again fail to do God's will; and His will is that we care for our brother as we previously wished him to care for us. Repentance calls for the enlistment of the individual in service to God. One has not repentance who does not find, as a result of that repentance, service to his fellow beings. Rather, this thought of repentance is a threat to many, to those who want ease and comfort in their human life and easy entry into the great kingdom of God. Yet repentance is the heart and soul of all spiritual growth and living.

Some avoid the threat of repentance by declaring that there is no sin and therefore, there is no real need of repentance. But we need to face up to sin and we must be certain that we understand just what sin is. Sin is not really the ethical and moral teaching which places restraints upon individuals by some so-called moral individuals or by political and religious organizations. Sin is merely self-centeredness. Whenever one thinks of himself more than he thinks of his fellow man, he is sinning. Sin is thinking of and acting upon the belief that one's own self, one's own comfort, one's own pleasures or one's own pain are the most important things to that individual. An individual who thinks that way is sinning.

In recent decades we have seen a watering down by the clergy and other religious teachers of the importance of this subject of repentance. The teaching often is that you can judge your closeness to God by the material things that you have acquired. And the teaching completely forgets Christ Jesus' teaching which is how much spirituality one has gained in his surrender of himself so that he can be of service to others. Often modern religion will erroneously judge one's spiritual growth by the material things, the riches that one gains. How often I have heard individuals say: "God was so good to me, He gave me a new Cadillac; He gave me a new fur coat." All this as a complete violation of Jesus' teaching about the evil of acquiring riches. He said: "How hardly shall they that have riches enter into the kingdom of God."

What mankind has called sin has changed from generation to generation, from decade to decade, sometimes from day to day. Often what we thought of as sin in childhood, we later found that it was not. I can remember listening to long discussions when I was a boy about the sin of women cutting their hair. We don't think that way any longer, yet I can remember that that was a very earnest question. And I can remember my father being very disturbed as women began to cut their hair. He thought it was a sin. Was it a sin? It was a belief that it was a sin, it was not a sin itself.

253

We've seen it in moral standards and in changes. Often many of our problems are caused because we are still holding on to what we think is a sin. There is but one sin, one great sin, one "real" sin. It always has been a sin; it will always remain a sin. And that one sin is to think about one's own self first. It is the sin of self-centeredness.

All of the human desire to change from self-centeredness to something better will not bring about repentance or even redemption. It requires returning to the redemptive power of God within. Christ Jesus' teaching and the teaching of all truly Holy Men have been that God resides or is kingdomed within individuals. One must, if he is to grow spiritually, repent of any selfish self-centeredness, for only through this repentance of self-centeredness can one find and live the redemptive power of Divinity within one's self.

Have you noticed this sense of redemptiveness which runs all the way through the Lord's Prayer where Jesus calls for a change? You are to care for your brothers as you would be cared for. You are to forgive another as you would be forgiven. Do you forgive another when they seem to be sometimes even causing great havoc in the human experience? Are you able to forgive them and to say: "Father, forgive them; for they know not what they do." Or do you criticize them and feel that you've got to change them? No, you've got to change your view about them, not them. Yet we often say: "If he just wouldn't do that everything would be so much better." Would it really? No, because the "so much better" has to come within one's Self. It has to come from that being of one's Self, experiencing one's own Identity.

Many fear this repentance. They say: "If I gave up my self-centeredness what would I have left!" If one truly gave it up he would have everything left. He would have his spiritual Self. One should not be afraid of the call of repentance, for repentance merely means an aspiration from God demanding that one be better and holier. Repentance is a call to acknowledge that the self-centeredness of one's former self is a transgression which must be set aside. We transgress upon our spiritual nature and that transgression must be set aside.

Repentance is not a call for us to look at ourselves as individuals born in sin and therefore must live a sinful life. Genuine repentance has no relationship to such self-loathing. Repentance does not call for self-hate, but for God-loving. Repentance is not self-centered, but actually a freedom from self-centeredness. It is that which enables us to regard God and the life He is demanding of us to be lived. One who lives the life of the selfless Self is living the life that is demanded by the teaching of repentance.

Repentance has actually nothing to do with the acknowledgement of our imagined sins —or maybe even what we believed to be real. Repentance is living the life of selfless service.

Or more accurately, it is calling us to be our Self so that we can live our life of selfless service. Then genuine repentance is much more than remorse for our past mistakes. Repentance is that which comes as a spiritual change in our thinking, our living and our being. It has to be more than just thinking of ourselves as a sinner and then acknowledging that sin and leaving it. It has to be more than just a truce with what we think of as being imaginary or our real sin.

So often individuals will say: "I know that I should change; I know that I should be doing this," or, "I will be doing it!" We say the words and we think that we've made a truce with our sin. But repentance is much more than just the truce with what we think of as our sin. Repentance is the rising up and going to the Father. It is the story of the Prodigal. It is the return to the love of the spiritual Father, to God Himself.

You are not responsible for anyone else's repentance. This is something that you must do yourself. How easy it is to say: "That person shouldn't be doing what he is doing." You cannot have genuine repentance when you are fidgeting about somebody else's spiritual development. You are responsible for only one individual's spiritual development and that is your own. It is this repentance which is the healing and saving power for mankind. And it doesn't require a great number of people engaged in it. In fact, if you have to tell even your closest friend about your repentance, you can be pretty sure that you have not taken part in the repentance. The repentance is that act which one engages in, in the closet experience. But it must be taken out of the closet into selfless service. Unless it is taken out of the closet in selfless service, it is not genuine repentance.

Very frequently I start our times together with one of Jesus' statements: "Where two or three are gathered together." It is the one, the two, the three, the small group that gathers together to do His will. In the New Testament it says "in my name" which means doing what he did. It is not a theological concept, although it has been misinterpreted as such. The "two or three gathered together" in his name are bringing together the redemptive work which they have done on themselves; and therefore, becoming a mighty force for healing, redeeming, saving.

It is the one who has repented that is able to become the "blessed" individual of the Beatitudes. "Blessed are the peacemakers." It is so easy to see that we don't have peace, we don't have prosperity, we don't have something because an individual "out there" or a group of individuals or another nation is doing some "thing" and they are responsible for the problems that we have. If you let yourself get into that thinking you will not be able to give to others in the full the redemptive healing power of God. There is no individual "out there," no group "out there," no nation "out there" that has power over you and your redemption.

257

Have you ever thought that the one whom you think erroneously about is not the one who needs redemption? How can they "touch" you if you are thinking evil about them, or thinking they are controlling your life or your neighbor's life or somebody else's life? The need is to purify yourself so that perhaps those very individuals that you have thought this about can "touch" you.

The redemptive power of God is not something that we declare, such as "I have repented," but it is the humility of willing to be washed in the River Jordan as Jesus was. Are you willing to go to the John the Baptist who thinks that he has to preach and talk about redemption? It is not arguing with him, not questioning him, but saying "suffer it to be so now."

The redemptive Power will always enable you to go and enter the River Jordan. It will not be something that you will be fighting about and saying: "That's not the highest thing, that's not the right thing, that's not the way to do it." You don't have to do that. It wasn't the highest thing for Jesus to be washed in the River Jordan. But if we have found within ourselves our own spiritual security we are not worried about the so-called backward steps.

We could easily argue: "Why did he have to do that?" The redemptive Power within himself gave him power so that he wasn't afraid of taking care of another's need. He didn't say: "That's not the right thing to do!"

258

Certainly it's not the right thing to do, but so often we say it's not the right thing and we move over to the wrong thing and from the wrong thing to the right thing. We move back and forth.

For spiritual development one must cease being self-centered. He must let the redemptive light of Divinity enlighten and change his mind, heart and life. Genuine repentance is the call to change from self-centeredness to the divine Self, to the God within.

Repentance is finding this divine Self as the motivating force for one's own thought, life and love.

XXXIII

DON'T AVOID THE STRUGGLE

Too long has the term sin and sinners been used as theological terms to explain the presence of sin and the one who engages in sin.

The organized Christian religion generally teaches that man by his nature is a sinner. We need to free ourselves from such a teaching. It's not true. Man, spiritual Man, that is, your genuine Identity, is free from what organized religion calls sin.

The Jewish/Christian religion has laid great emphasis upon the essential necessity of recognizing what sin is and the handling of sin. But let no one fool himself. If one is going to advance spiritually he must understand the very importance of recognizing what sin is and the handling of sin. We need to look squarely at this teaching regarding sin and see the way that it has been interpreted by the Jewish/Christian tradition which lacks Divine authority.

260

We should ask ourselves just what sin is. I'm going to give you a definition of sin, the only valid definition of sin, but not the definition that is usually given. Correctly understood, sin is but the failure to live up to the highest in you. Every time you fail to live up to the highest in you, you are engaging in sin. It is that sin, that failure, that you need to overcome.

Sin, as I am using the term, is the state of mind which, ignorantly or consciously, believes in a separation between one's self and his God. You are not a sinner because you violate some moral or ethical law, you are a sinner (if I can use the word sinner) only when you fail to live up to your spiritual greatness, when you fail to live up to your oneness with your God.

Sin is not something that you have to avoid, nor do you have to be worried that you are going to commit a sin. It's not a violation of an ethical or moral law, or a theological concept. It is merely a failure; and viewing it as a failure, then one is able to grapple with it and handle it.

Sin is the failure to recognize one's own spiritual greatness. It's the failure to recognize one's oneness with the divine Being, and having recognized that greatness and that oneness, failing to express it. Basically you must accept the fact that you are not a sinner nor is anyone else a sinner, that is, not as the term is used theologically. It is merely the failure to discover and to live up to your highest spiritual Self.

You will never get rid of sin in all the teachings and obedience to the teachings that creates in you or in someone else, a fear that you are a sinner and must sin. You will never get rid of it by believing that it is some "thing." You will never get rid of it by believing that it is you. You are not a sinner. You are one with the God-power; and one who is one with the God-power cannot be defined as a sinner.

You don't have to worry about somebody else's sin, another nation's sin. It's not the sin that your parents engaged in or that you feel they may have engaged in. It's not sin passed on to the third and fourth generation as referred to in the Old Testament.

It's so easy to think that somebody else is a failure. You may have heard the story of the father who had a son who had not been very good. When the father came home that evening the mother said: "Will you speak to Johnny?" And the father said to him: "Your mother and I have spent so much time with you. We have worked and worked and you are still rude and naughty." And the boy looked at the father and said: "What a failure you are!"

They had spent time and they had failed. The child could not see that the problem was his problem. How easy it is to blame others instead of looking squarely at ourselves. The great battle, the great Armageddon, is not a battle between two forces out there some place, external from yourself. The only

Armageddon that you will engage in is the battle between two internal forces, the force that prompts you to do good and the force that prompts you to do evil.

The great battle of Armageddon is not a battle between nations between, say, the United States and the Soviet Union. Armageddon is an internal battle. It is the battle with yourself, to free yourself from your failure to be and to live your spiritual greatness. And one of those battles is to free yourself from the belief that you are a sinner.

We must realize that we have the power to be what God created us to be. All this makes us stop and think: "What did God create us to be?" He created us to be His chosen vessel—to share His love with His creation and creatures. To be God-in-action. To be His love. To be His care. To be His abundant, sustaining Force—to express our love to others.

How very easy it may seem to believe that there is an evil person called satan or the devil which makes you do evil. You may remember that comedian who used to say: "The devil made me do it!" How easy it is to think that it's something or someone else. If we can't think of a person who makes us do wrong or another nation that makes us do wrong, we create a devil that makes us do wrong. Actually the devil is a creation of the human mind so that the human mind doesn't have to face up to its own lack of validity.

By believing in a satan we are enabled to avoid the responsibility which is ours, the responsibility to face up to our own acts. But there is no satan. There is only failure. And it is not someone else's failure that you have to be concerned about. It is your own failure. You cannot blame your failure on anyone. You can't blame it on society. You can't blame it on conditions into which you were born. You can't blame it on another nation. You are the one who has within yourself the God-power to rise above failure, to be what you've been created to be.

In a theological sense I have said that sin is unreal, but you accomplish nothing by going around and declaring the unreality of sin. Sin has to be accepted, but it must be accepted merely as failure. Even that which organized religion calls sin can be successfully handled by overcoming failure, overcoming that which is in you that keeps you from service to God's creatures and creation.

Sin is not an offense against God. The only sin is the offense against our fellow creatures. It is the offense of failure, failure to express our own salvation through service to others.

We are not punished for our failures, we are punished by our failures. It is through the darkness of our struggles with failure that we see clearly the divine Light. To spend time needlessly feeling guilty over present or past sins (imagined or what we may even think to be real) is time wasted. We are not called to waste time, we are called to be "doers." We are not called to wallow in the mire of sin, we are called to do things. We are not called to the mire of even the guilt of sin.

The struggle to overcome this battle of Armageddon is something that you must engage in. You need to engage in it, you can engage in it, but you do not have to create the power to engage in that battle. That Power has already been given to you by the God-power within yourself.

We need to be up and doing. We need an awareness of who we are. And who are we? We're God's chosen one, sharing our selfless love with all. One who is sharing his selfless love with all is certainly not a sinner.

XXXIV

IN THE WILDERNESS

We all need to engage in labor, in a constructive sense of labor. By labor I mean the struggling that is a struggle with one's self. For without constructive struggle there can be — indeed, there is no spiritual growth.

This need of struggle is illustrated in the life of every spiritual Teacher who has ever trod this planet. And this struggle is also true in the life of the Master Christian, Christ Jesus. Have you ever thought that before he gave his constructive and wonderful Sermon on the Mount, according to Matthew, he struggled, he had strife, he met temptation. And all this took place in the wilderness.

The words of the gospel writer says that he went "into the wilderness to be tempted of the devil." He went to be tempted. He went for the strife. He knew that struggle was important for him if he was to continue on the

266

course that he had set for himself—the course of spiritual development and spiritual work.

Jesus willingly allowed himself to be tempted. Are you willing to allow yourself to be tempted? Are you willing to face up to the struggle which comes into your life? Such facing up to the struggle is the surest way, the only valid way for advancing spiritually. When we avoid the facing up to strife, we stifle spiritual development. We must be willing to go into the wilderness of despair, loneliness, unhappiness—and in that wilderness to be tempted.

To avoid the wilderness struggle is to deprive ourselves of our closeness with the divine Source, that divine Source which comforts and sustains us in our struggling experiences, in our difficult times. Like the Master Christian, we must willingly allow ourselves to be tempted by the devil.

It's so easy to say: "There is no devil!" Where is the devil? What is the devil? The devil is that negative belief which imprisons us in the concept that we are less than what we are, that we are less than the child in us. Let's put it another way—that we are less than at-one with the divine Source of our being. This negative belief, this devil is only a belief which must be wrestled with if we are to find our own individual Peniel.

By Peniel I am referring to the Old Testament character who struggled with himself. He would not let the angel message, the spiritual message that came to him, would not let it go until it blessed him, until he found his blessing in the struggle. The narrative then says that Jacob named the place Peniel because he had seen God face to face. We should not cease our struggle until we see our Peniel, until we see our God face to face, until we see our oneness with our God.

To avoid the struggle, individuals do it in so many different ways. They say "I won't visit with that person because there's always a struggle when I do. I won't have anything to do with that particular religious denomination. I won't have anything to do with that political party because whenever I do there's a struggle." But to avoid that struggle is to deprive one's self of one's individual Peniel.

There's always been this negative belief; and there is this negative belief of separation today. But this negative belief, this devil, must be faced up to and overcome; and it is for that reason that one walks through this human experience. We need to take our stand against this negative belief, this devil, and see it fall by the weight of its own falsity. We do not struggle against an enemy that has power; it has only the power that our beliefs give to it. But it is necessary that we see that it is a belief.

It was necessary for Jesus at the beginning of his ministry, to face up to the struggle with the belief in the validity and reality of material life as all important. If you are having difficulty finding your missionary purpose in life, it may well be that you have not yet faced up to the belief that material life is all important, that it has validity and reality.

This is not a struggle that can be imposed upon you by an authority outside yourself. It cannot be imposed upon you by government, by parents or even by a religious teaching or a Teacher. It is not a struggle demanded by society or organized religion. It is a struggle which you agree with yourself to engage in, for it is a struggle with yourself. It is the struggle which enables you to accept and be what you have been created to be, and to express that spiritual Force in your daily human lives.

This struggle, faced up to, enables you to be a mighty force for spiritual good. It saves you and frees you from self-serving good. It will save you from being the one who is always doing good but is always letting everybody know how much good you are doing.

Facing up to this struggle will free you from voicing "vain repetitions" which, in presenting truths to others, you imagine the repetitions to be truth. You declare the words to be truths. You say to others that they should be doing this and this or they should not be doing this and this; and you present the words as if they were true. When you struggle with yourself you will see that there's no need to engage in such vain repetitions which you declare to be true.

There's no point in having a struggle and leaving it there; it has to be faced up to. Through the struggle faced up to, you yourself become the Word of God on earth. The words of all organization—and it doesn't matter which organized religion—will vanish away, for no organized religion will endure forever. Only the Word—that is, the Word of God expressed in you and as You—exists forever.

This Word of God is untouched by human birth or human death. It's untouched by what organized religion says or does not say. It is untouched by what society says or does not say. This Word of God, this you that has been redeemed by the struggle, exists as the spiritual You. And it can only be found within your Self.

Let the Word speak to you and it will speak clearest to you during the struggle. There in the wilderness your God will speak directly and clearly to you. In that wilderness, in that struggle, you will be aware that you are His beloved, His beloved in whom He is "well pleased."

The Word spoke clearest to Jesus during his temptation and during his time on the cross —during his struggle experience. The Word will speak to you if you are but willing to go into the wilderness, if you are willing to free yourself from the concept of an abundance of things. Those things do not necessarily have to be material things, they may be things such as what you think are spiritual teachings of a church or the demands of society. The struggle is to free yourself from the abundance of things.

It is the desire for things, for place, for a healthy body that you must struggle with. It's the desire you struggle with, not the things themselves. There in the wilderness, because of your struggle, you are free from the desire for things, free from the desire for an honored place in society, free even from the desire for a good human body. There in the wilderness you stand alone, at-one with the creative Source of your very being.

It is not the abundance of things that must be laid aside, it is the belief in the importance and reality of things which, through great struggle, must be given up. Free yourself from the belief that the abundance of possessions such as human knowledge, material things and so-called religious teaching are important to your well-being. Jesus had to prove, as we have to prove, that human pride and material abundance must be seen for what they are—a snare that binds us, a snare which prevents us from running the race of spiritual development.

Even more important to your spiritual development than the times when you feel you have gained spiritual illumination are the times of willingness to struggle which you have in the wilderness. How often individuals will say to me: "I had such a wonderful spiritual illumination!" I wouldn't belittle that spiritual illumination, but I would say that they are not nearly as important as the willing struggle in the wilderness of one's own being.

271

You need not be free from human living to be what you have been created to be. So often individuals say: "When I have a great deal of spiritual development, then I will do this." You don't get spiritual development without the struggle. And you do not struggle with things, but the desire for and the dependence upon things.

Don't ask for things for yourself. Don't even pray for things for yourself. Pray for spiritual growth. Pray to be led into the wilderness, away from the self-satisfying dependence on things. It is not the things that are the problem, it is the dependence upon things. This willing struggle is vastly important to you and for you. Willingly engaged in the sturggle. If and when you do, you will find that you have been engaging in a struggle with a foe that has only imagined power.

The struggle will enable you to see that all reality is to be found in the spiritual Realm, not in the things possessed. It is to be found in the living of this spiritual life, and living in this spiritual life in the realm we call human life. If it is not lived in the human it's not being lived at all.

The struggle will enable you to be the Word of God Itself, to voice that Word of God and to heal by that Word of God. Through the struggle you become the Word, and this Word is the Force that will ultimately enable you to bring redemption into the lives of others.

Through the struggle you will see that all you need is to be found in and as your forever oneness with the divine Reality of your being. Through the struggle you will be at peace in the Peniel of your own spiritual life.

XXXV

CARING FOR GOD'S OWN

Love is one of the most respected and hallowed words in the English language; and while love is a respected and honored word it is probably one of the most misunderstood of words.

What one thinks of love as given to us by Divinity is not what love actually is. Love is more than words. Love is more than a passive, indifferent declaration that "God is love," or even "I love you." Love is the actual living, being and doing of love.

The Greek word for the highest, the purest and the most selfless expression of love is Agape. So that we will not have a misunderstanding, I am using the expression Agape-love. In one sense this is not a good use of these words because Agape means love— as if I were saying Love-love. But I'm using this expression Agape-love to distinguish it from that which parades as love.

Agape-love is that sense of love that is God-given and is valid only when it is used as selfless service to others. It is not the love that people so often think about when they say "God loves" and we think of something that God is going to give to us. Agape-love is God expressing Himself through you, through me and through others. Agape-love, this higher sense of love, is the love given by God and must be expressed. It is not something that you learn or talk about and it certainly is not something that you can barter. We may think of love as almost something that is bartered, something that we can buy, but love is none of those things. Love is the free giving of God's mercy, care and abundance to others.

Selfless love, Agape-love, is love freely given — and equally important — it must be equally accepted. It is necessary that you not only give love but that you cultivate the ability to accept love because it is a complete cycle—love given, love received. So often we want to receive love but we are not prepared to give love. We want to give love but we don't accept love when it is given to us. We say: "Here's some money for the love that you are expressing towards me." That is not Agape-love.

Agape-love is not a spiritual abstraction called love. Agape-love is divine Love at work between human beings. Agape-love is not you selfishly giving love, saying: "I don't really want to give love," but you give it just because it's required of you. Agape-love is God's manifestation of His love expressed by

275

one human being to God's creatures and creation.

In the parable of the Good Samaritan, how did the Samaritan find his God? He found Him in service to someone in need. You can never find God except as a Samaritan. Only as you give Samaritan-like service to someone in need do you have your God.

Agape-love, then, is the love of God caring for another where the other finds himself. How often you say: "I'd love to take care of that individual, to help him if he would do so and so"—just change some way. But that's not good enough. It would be like the Samaritan coming along and finding this fellow by the side of the road and saying: "I'd love to help that fellow if he were just standing up straight or if he could get on the animal that I have here." You help where you find the other.

Agape-love demands that you love another where he is, not where you think he should be. Above all, we must help those who think they have fallen by the wayside; because in helping those who have fallen, we are actually helping ourselves spiritually, but we shouldn't do it for this reason. Those in need are your saviors. Those in need of healing, of housing, of food, of friendship—they are the ones who will save you from being just a mortal and will enable you to be what you have been created to be, God-in-action.

Your love is not based upon what another considers love, but what comes out of your own inner Awareness of the God who is Agape-love. Love must prompt us to do what is proper and correct—doing the right things to care for our brother. Love is not sitting back and waiting for the time when we will be of service or rushing around smartly so that we have no time for our spiritual development.

There is a sense of service that rushes around and takes care of this person, takes care of that person. But let me caution you against a negative sense of service. It doesn't come out of that stillness of having spiritually grown. There can be no sense of over-service or under-service. There is only the normalcy of service and God expresses Himself through normalcy. It is normal for man to be of service.

Read the Gospels again and notice how often Jesus talks about taking care of those in need —healing the sick, raising the dead, cleansing the lepers, and doing so without any sense of recompense. Jesus demanded service and there is no obedience to God without obedience to God's demand that you serve His creatures and creation in need.

To care for our brother in a way that we, sometimes in our own self-righteousness, feel that he should be taken care of is not enough. There must be practical, human care and that practical, human care must be balanced in a sense of having found that care within one's self. Out of that care within one's self we express the right human action that seems right under the condition in which we find ourself. In fact the one who is closest to Divinity will discern best the practical need of another.

Sometimes love-in-action demands an action that the one to whom your love is being expressed may feel that it is not love. For instance, a parent has to be sure that a child learns obedience and sometimes has to do things that the child does not consider loving. A parent is not expressing his Agape-love for a child by permitting him to do whatever he selfishly thinks he wants to do and what is right in his eyes. Such a parent must resist such selfish acts on the part of the offspring. God inspired resistance to evil, evil expressed by a child, is one of the ways in which Agape-love is expressed.

Agape-love is not something you understand. Agape-love is beyond understanding. You cannot gain an understanding about Agape-love. Individuals will say: "I'm trying to express it correctly," and they are talking about putting things into a correct form of saying something. But Agape-love is already operating as love between one human and another. It is always expressing itself as love for one's neighbor. It is up to each of you and to me to express this love which is already in operation. For it is only in love for our neighbor that we can actually show our love to God.

How do you find God? You don't find Him in a Teacher. You don't find Him in a teaching. And you won't find God in a church. You may think you do, but actually you find God in a brother in need. Because when you find a brother in need, you then have the wonderful opportunity of expressing Agape-love. And everyone you encounter throughout the day is a brother in need.

Through the many years that I have been teaching spiritual Truth, I have often had individuals come to me and say: "I want to love God more!" And when it was pointed out that the only way to love God is to love what God has created, they said: "But that's an abstraction. I want to love God!" Actually their concept of loving God is the abstraction, because you can see people that need love, you can care for someone who needs you.

You cannot really love the God whom you not only do not see but cannot see unless you have already loved your neighbor whom you can see. In the Bible, the question is asked: How can he who does not love his brother whom he sees, love God whom he does not see? And the answer of course is that he cannot. If one is spending his time away from the world, away from conflict, then he is not expressing Agape-love. Agape-love has to be expressed in contact with others; and it is only in the conflict with others that we find the God who is the source of Agape-love.

Agape-love is the loving of our brother in God, and God in our brother. Applied humanly, this love must be expressed realistically. It must be in keeping with the needs of the one who needs help. But I hasten to add that you do not as a human person create the Agape-love that you are to express. Agape-love is God's own love—God Himself loving—expressed through you and as you. You live and move and have your being in God and in His love, but not the way in which you think you want to love. It is in His love that you express Divinity.

It is the love of God which enables us to love our neighbor and to love ourselves in the same light. Loving ourselves is loving a neighbor; and when we love our neighbor, we love ourselves. They're one and the same light from Divinity, the same enlightenment which shines from the divine Source Itself.

What does it mean to love another? Does it mean just to go around and patch up a physical body, to provide a home for someone? These may well be the outward signs, but actually to love another is to fully see God in that other individual.

You are not called upon just to take care of the bodily needs of another or the spiritual needs of another. You are called upon to take care of both the spiritual needs and the bodily needs. It is to see another as he truly is and to see him in two ways as one—both as a bodily entity and a spiritual entity—expressing himself wholly and completely. When you see that in another you are loving.

It is important that you do not place certain things as holy and other things such as service as not so holy. You say "Praying is holy and spiritual, but caring for a sick, sinning, dying individual is not quite as holy." That's not true. Care is care, love is love, no matter what you are doing. A parent teaching a babe to walk is a holy experience. A person helping a dope addict or a drunkard or what someone might call an immoral person—to help such an individual is a holy act, providing it is not done in the sense of: "I have found my way, therefore you have to find your way." There can be no self-aggrandizement in Agape-love.

Each and every act of Agape-love which finds its source in divine Love is in its way as valid and important as any other act. So often individuals say: "I wish I could get to where I no longer have to take care of others." You'll never reach such a point. You'll never outgrow your own individual need to love. To love is your continual and sacred responsibility. To love means to accept new challenges daily in your service to your brother.

You may say: "What's the great thing that I need for my spiritual growth?" You need to accept a new and deeper awareness of your responsibility to serve God and to realize that you can serve Him in no other way than to serve those in need around you. You have no other way of serving Him.

Agape-love is selfless giving and selfless receiving. It is the willingness to be what we

281

have been created to be, selfless servants in the Father's vineyard—caring for God's own. Selfless service is caring for God's people.

XXXVI

GOD'S GIFT IS HIMSELF

[This talk was preceded by the reading of the 13th Chapter of First Corinthians and the first verse of the 14th.]

As I was reading that 13th Chapter of First Corinthians I could almost hear some of you saying: "Not another talk on love!" And perhaps that's what we usually do—we talk of love.

We think about love. We wish for love. We read romantic stories about love. We see motion pictures dealing with the question of love. And we are told in that wonderful book by Drummond that "The greatest thing in the world is love."

Religious leaders are constantly telling us about the virtues of love. Sometimes even political leaders ask people to love one another. Yet with all this talk about love, all this coercing of man to think in terms of love, why do we still have war? Why is one race of man killing another race of man? Why is one economic group taking advantage of another economic group? Why is one nation trying to put itself above another? Why is it that the hungry are not fed, the sick are not comforted, the unloved remain unloved?

Of course the answers to these questions are multifaceted and there are many answers; but certainly one of the answers is that there is too much talk about love and not enough loving. The word love has become a meaningless cliché. We talk of love and yet we do not realize that love has to be more than a word called love. Perhaps we should exchange the word love for the word loving.

Love as a word is meaningless; it has no healing power—no redemptive power. We can talk love till the end of time, yet it is but "sounding brass, or a tinkling cymbal" which profiteth nothing. The word love as a word is powerless to do good.

What we need is a new and holy definition of the word love, to redefine what we think of as love. We should "undefine" love (and I know there's no such word as undefine). In fact, if we understood what we mean by God as love we would undefine God; because God is not a word called love nor is He a person who loves.

We put on that word love what we think is loving. We glibly say that "God is love." But at the same time we fail to realize that this love which is God is more than a word or a definition of God. When we say "God is love," it should mean something more to us than just a glib statement. When we say "God is love," we should mean that God is expressing in us, through our sharing of His goodness and reality, His love with others. God is love has to be more than a statement, an affirmation or even a prayer. God is love has to be a loving.

Love is the Divine process of God sharing Himself. It is God loving. But how does God love? What is His sharing? What is His "method" of sharing, His method of loving? His method of loving is through us being His love-in-action. He has no other way of sharing or being love than through you, through me and others as loving.

Usually we think of love as something that we give to another, that we barter with another, that if we love someone we at least hope that that one will give us love back. We think of love as a commodity that is given and received. Nothing could be further from the truth. Love isn't some thing. Love is the Divine process of uniting with another—with his pain, his pleasures, his successes, his failures, his joys and his sadness. Unless there is that uniting there is not really genuine Love.

We need to get rid of the idea that love is a commodity, something that we give to others, something which we share with others. But it is God sharing through His creation, through you, through me. God is love in you because you have the Divine right to be love-in-action. God is love in you as you share His love—as you are loving.

Love isn't something that you give to another. It's not even something that you give to God. It's something bigger than that. Love is being the God of love in daily living. Love is being God in our every thought and action, in our every step through life. Loving is not giving another what is commonly thought of as love. It is loving another by seeing in him the God who is love.

How often you hear people say: "My happiest time was when I was in love." And later they will say: "The most destructive thing that ever happened to me was when I was in love and love disappeared or failed." What we need to be in love with is loving, sharing, giving—taking part in that Divine process of love.

Through the years that I have done spiritual counseling, I've had many people tell me about the great energy and time they spend in trying to find love, failing to realize that love can't be found. You can search till the end of time and you will never find love, because Love can only be lived. Love can only be lived as God-in-action.

What the world needs are those who are willing to be their divine Self through seeing in another or in others, God Himself. For it is in loving your brother—that is, the selfless loving of your divine Self—that you are able to selflessly share.

Christ Jesus instructed his followers to love their neighbor as themselves. And you are called upon to love your neighbor, whether that neighbor lives next door to you or halfway around the world. Loving your neighbor as yourself is to love your neighbor as you love your spiritual, divine, holy Self.

You have to be willing to let the self-centered self with all of its wants, its desires, cares and its willfulness die. It's not good enough to love your neighbor as your self-centered self. You love your neighbor as your divine Self, so that you can glory in another, knowing that in another you find your Self. If you spend time trying to understand yourself— that is, your lower self, your self-centered self —you will never be able to love your neighbor. To love your Self is to forget your self-centered self in selfless service to others.

Love is no respecter of persons whatsoever. Loving your neighbor is loving all people and making no exceptions. And it is especially true that we need to love our enemies. It takes very little spiritual insight or stamina to love your family or your friends, but it takes great spiritual courage to love your enemies.

Perhaps we make that word enemy mean what we think of as an enemy in war. But the word enemy actually means those whom you do not respect, that you don't see something of God in them. It is seeing something of God in that one whom you cannot see something of God in, which spells your spiritual growth. It's

in the loving of your enemies that the greatest
of spiritual growth is always to be found.

It's not so much that you love God or
that God loves you, but that you are loving,
that you are the love of God expressing love
to all, and especially to your enemies. You
are to be God's loving presence and help to
all. By loving you exchange the word love for
the Divine activity of loving.

We must love all God's creatures and
creation. We are to love all—from the tiny
mustard seed to the expansive universe. We are
to love everything—every animal, every plant,
every tree, every person. You have been
created to walk through this experience for but
one purpose and that purpose is so that you
will love.

So much of what parades as love, that
talks about the need to "love yourself," is all
the time thinking of the human self and will
never enable you or anyone else to find love,
much less to find God through the living of
love. It is only as you let the self-willed self
die that the divine Self can come forth. And
that divine Self asks for nothing for Itself
because the Self needs nothing.

Only as that self dies and there is the
rebirth of the divine Self will you be Love-in-
action, will you have a kinship with the awareness that God is love. Finding and living love is
the only experience of being born again.
Loving your neighbor as you love your divine
Self enough so that you can love another is

taking part in the only genuine rebirth, the rebirth of living the selfless Self.

Feel the exhilerating mystery of being the love of God. By loving, you take part in the spiritual and divine Mystery of life, the Divine activity of loving. As you are loving you will find that you are free from the platitudes about love. You will be Love Itself and being Love Itself is being divine Love-in-action.

As love-in-action you can share the greatest gift in the world, divine Love. I've almost ended by saying that love is a gift; and if we're not careful we'll think of the gift as some thing that we give. But when you give a gift to another, the gift is a hollow, unimportant gift unless it has behind it the unction of Love.

God's gift is not a thing. God's gift is Himself—expressing Himself through you and as You.

XXXVII

PRAYER IN THE GREEN ROOM

When we are prone to think about somebody as less than God-created or think of a group of people or maybe a nation as less than God-created, we need to go to our own individual Green room; and we all have a Green Room.

In the older theatres there was usually a room called "The Green Room." Sadly, these rooms are not being built in the modern theatres. Most of the actors prefer to have their visitors come and see them in their dressing rooms. But in the older theatres there were these Green Rooms where the actors would wait for their cues or where they would receive visitors after the performances.

Frequently I have attended performances in the theatre and then through the years have gone backstage to meet the actors. I can remember when I have seen an actor play the meanest character that you could possibly imagine; and then when I would go back and visit with him afterwards he would be very cordial, kind and considerate, quite unlike the character he had played.

Many times since then I have thought that this is very much like prayer. It is freeing us from the "actor," the thing we see and believe to be a person. We believe him to be unkind, unloving and thoughtless. When that occurs why don't we go into our Green Room and see the true individuality of that person?

Many people feel that the Green Room is so-called because it was originally painted green. But originally the room was a place for storing scenery. The actors waited in the scene room and met their guests there. Very probably green is a corruption of the word "scene," and the scene room became known as the Green Room. As an actor has a Green Room where he may entertain his guests, so each of us has his room—his realm of spiritual awareness—where he may joyously entertain the spiritual messages from Divinity.

How much of your life do you spend in acting? You see Mrs. Jones coming down the street and you say: "She will want me to do such and such; she will want me to be cheerful." So you put on an outward sense of cheerfulness. Or, "I see Mr. Smith coming down the street and I don't like him," so you act in a certain way because you don't like him. You play act. You avoid somebody because you don't get along with them. Again, it's acting. Don't be a play actor.

291

You are called upon to live your life in relationship to doing good to everyone, not acting. You can't do it by just doing good human deeds alone. The good human deeds have to come out of something within yourself, a spiritual development within yourself. Otherwise, you become one who just again is acting, acting a role of a do-gooder. Doing good has to come out of being spiritually aware.

You may be thinking: Just where is this Green Room? Jesus tells us plainly where it is. He said: "When thou prayest, enter into thy closet." It is the closet of spiritual Awareness. If we will go into our closet and see the person that we thought of as less than God-created, we will be doing something constructive. On the other hand it is not constructive if we keep believing in the action that the person may be engaging in—the same as the actor on the stage who is engaging in actions that are not very becoming.

As we grow Spiritward we have to be willing to look beyond the actor to the true Identity of every individual and every group of people that cross our path. All of this made me think of Jesus' instructions about prayer given in the Sermon on the Mount. The Sermon was gathered by Matthew to express the teachings of Jesus. Whether it was a sermon as such we do not know for certain; but it certainly was a gathering together of the basic teachings of Jesus. And if you want to know the basic teachings of Jesus read the Sermon on the Mount. The interesting thing about this

292

Sermon is that all the instructions are a doing experience. The prayer that it mentions is far from abstractions. There's nothing in the prayer about abstractions.

We must place our concept of prayer where Jesus mentions the prayer; and if we place it in the Sermon on the Mount, it becomes a doing rather than just sitting down in an abstract, theoretical way pleading to God. In fact, if you look up the definition of prayer you will find such words as entreating and pleading. That is the usual concept of prayer, but there is nothing like that in Jesus' concept of prayer.

Prayer, if it is spiritual prayer, will inevitably bring about what those looking on call action. It will never permit one to live in a negative sense of aloneness. Prayer by its very nature demands that there be action. It demands that those who pray must heal the sick, raise the dead, cleanse the lepers. In short, prayer is the free giving back to the Source which has freely given to the individual. Only such prayer that brings action is spiritual prayer.

Prayer should not be so much a talking to God as it is letting the God in you see the God in another. And to see it despite what evidence may appear to the five physical senses about that individual. Prayer must be the doing of good to others. All so-called prayer that does not manifest itself as goodness to others is what I would call negative prayer or a misconception of prayer.

In referring to Jesus' instructions about prayer, I'm going to use the Phillips translation of the New Testament which I think brings out more clearly what Jesus actually meant. We have drawn up around the King James Version almost a "holy" sense of things—not the right sense of holy as being very sacred, but it has become negatively sacred.

Sometimes we need to be jarred into the fact that prayer is something which we engage in every single day in a very practical way. For instance, we are acquainted with the statement in the Sermon on the Mount that says "Judge not, that ye be not judged." The Phillips Translation says: "Don't criticize people, and you will not be criticized."

Basic to prayer is freedom from criticism. You can't criticize a person, because the thing that you see wrong in him is not him. It is the actor on the stage of life. If you are tempted to criticize somebody, get rid of that criticism before you try to pray. Because if you pray with criticism you will not be able to enter your Green Room. You will not be able to enter that closet. Free yourself from criticism, from judging.

You may say: "I don't criticize people." But do you sometimes think "That's the best which that person can do," or, "What can you expect from such a person?" Notice what the translator says: "Don't criticize people and you will not be criticized." But perhaps you say: "I have often not criticized people and I have been criticized." The one that is not going to

294

criticize you will be God. It will not be the person. You may get criticism, but God will criticize you until you stop criticizing others. Now this is rather hard to take if you think of God as a person, but if you see Him as spirit you won't have that problem.

Jesus talks about not giving audible prayers. Prayer is to be something that is so sacred with you that you can't even give it audibly. The usual concept of prayer is often the audible prayer, given in a church or in a synagogue. Jesus is talking about an entirely different concept of prayer. He talks about those who pray and make a big thing out of it and he says that's all the reward they will get.

Jesus gave very definite instructions as to what prayer is to be. It is interesting how he starts this discussion of how to pray. The very first thing he says is: "When you do good to other people." The basis of all prayer is doing good to other people. Spiritual prayer is not saying: "God, send me a new fur coat" or, "Get me out of this situation in which I've found myself." Sometimes we've placed ourselves there by our own foolishness. It's not any of those things.

In this case Jesus was talking about alms and he is leading up to the question of prayer. And he said: "When you pray, go into your own room, shut your door and pray to your Father privately." There really isn't such a thing as community prayers, not even church prayers, not as Jesus defines it. The only legitimate prayer is the prayer that is private.

Other prayers may have their place and may help you, but eventually all prayer has to be the entering of your Green Room. Prayer is entering into your closet and there shutting the door—on judging your fellow man, criticizing or thinking of anyone less than God's creation. And I don't care what that person has done or is doing at that very moment. He may be what the world would call "a miserable sinner," but unless you go into your closet and shut that door of criticism, of judging or thinking someone is less than what you are, you have not prayed.

When you pray, go into your own room. How big is your room? "In my Father's house are many rooms. I go to prepare a room for you." Do you know that there's a room prepared for you and that room is the room of your own spiritual Awareness? You've got to go in and find your own Identity, your own individual spiritual Awareness. That's entering the room. All of Jesus' teaching was to enable individuals to enter their own room. He couldn't go into the room for individuals, but He encouraged them to go into the room. That's all a spiritual Teacher can do for anyone.

We've been talking about going into the closet and you would think that if you went into the closet alone, that if you would accept the usual definition of aloneness it would be "My Father which art in heaven." But his closet, the closet that Jesus talked about, the room that you are going into, is being alone with God and all that He creates so that your prayer is a prayer of brotherhood.

Jesus says that genuine prayer is entering your closet. There you will be alone with your own love of others, because your aloneness includes all. If you are not alert you'll think that he's saying: "Go in there and shut out the world." But your aloneness includes all and will manifest itself if you've actually prayed, as action in the human experience. If you've prayed as Jesus and other Holy Men have instructed you to pray, it will be manifested in action towards others.

Jesus sets the stage and he says: "When you pray, don't be like the play actor who is on the stage. He's mean, he's corrupt, he's not living a genuine life. He's living a playacting life." Then he said: "When you pray don't rattle off long prayers." I've had people say to me: "You know I've prayed for an hour on this thing!" Probably they rattled off long prayers for an hour. There can be no rattling of prayers, because prayer is the living force of doing good to others. Without that doing of good to others there is no prayer. If your prayer doesn't prompt goodness to others, you have not prayed.

We have perverted the prayer into a ritual by reciting it so often; whereas, the prayer itself must be the reclaiming of our unity with God and all that He creates. Anything less is not prayer. I'll tell you a little secret. As you grow in this type of prayer you will not have to say: "I've got to set aside this time" and give long, worded prayers. You'll pray right while you're doing other things. You'll be touched whether you're washing your dishes or mowing a lawn.

Jesus said that you are not rewarded for your many words and that God who is your Father knows your needs before you ask him. Then why do you tell God about your needs? To pray for health or success, it's a waste of time. If God already knows, it's His duty to care for you, to sustain you. Then why do you have to tell Him that He's not doing it now and to hurry up and give you some good? Your Father already knows your needs.

Jesus gave an example of a prayer, but that prayer was not to become "the" prayer. He does not say to use these words, but almost as if he is saying: "Pray something like this." I have a feeling that he gave a very simple, humble prayer; and if you ponder the Biblical Greek there is no indication that he said to pray this prayer.

What was this prayer that Jesus gave? It's more than words. It was instruction and he did not intend that it be rattled off. In fact, it's almost as if he said: "Don't be tricked into using this prayer as if it has something special in it." The only thing that will be special will be the reformation within your own life. If you will use the Lord's Prayer as instruction rather than as a prayer that you feel has some magic in it, because you can recite it so well, it can be of great help to you. But it shouldn't become a ritual to you.

"Our Father" is a prayer in which we all have one mutual Father. So that the people wouldn't think in terms of the Jewish thought of the times, where the human father was the

298

head of a family, Jesus tells which Father it is. It's the higher concept of Father, so he calls it "heavenly Father," not that God is in a place called heaven, but that He is above the usual concept of father.

"Our heavenly Father, may your name be honored." How do you honor God's name? There's only one way that you can honor God's name and it's by honoring those whom you can see with your eyes. You'll never be able to see God with your eyes; you have to honor God through the individuals you come in contact with each and every day. There's no other way of honoring this "Our Father." Since He is "Our Father," you have to see beyond the actor that you have been tempted to believe in— either your own self as an actor or somebody else acting out a role—and see the God and the good in that individual.

You have to see beyond the covering, to use an expression that Thomas uses (in the Gospel According to Thomas). The covering is that which individuals put over themselves to defend themselves against what they think of as the world's anger, by sometimes building a defense of not being interested in other people. We've got to be able to see beyond the covering to where we honor the individual as God-in-action. You certainly pray that you will express God. Then why shouldn't you feel that your brother is also God-in-action? Your prayer is to see the God in another and to see despite the coverings he may have that he has placed over himself or you have placed over him.

299

"Our heavenly Father, may your name be honored." What kind of name are you giving to people with whom you come in contact? Do you name them sometimes as stupid; do you name them as an aggressor; do you name them as sick? This prayer is a prayer that is enabling you to be God-in-action. Anything less than that is not genuine prayer. So when you see the actor rather than the true Identity of the individual you are violating your prayer.

You can test pretty well how your prayers have been. It's not going to be how long you have prayed or how much truth you've gathered up even if you've gathered it up from an inspired Teacher; but it's how much good you are doing to others. Prayer is doing good for other people.

Jesus' whole premise here is on "When thou doest." In fact, the whole of the Sermon on the Mount is how to get along with others, how to do good for them that despitefully use you and persecute you. How often individuals have said to me: "I wish that person wouldn't belittle me!" Instead, one should use that belittling as a wonderful opportunity for spiritual development. It is only in conflict with your misconception of other people that you will find spiritual development. There's no other way.

Won't you take time to go into your Green Room? Before you retire tonight will you ask yourself how much acting you did today. How much genuine living did you do? And I will tell you how you will know how much

300

genuine living you did, because it will be manifested in human action towards doing good to another.

Stop looking at the actor all the time. Go into your Green Room and there pray to your Father. And the only way you can pray to your Father is to correct the misconceptions. Lift yourself above the misconceptions that you see of the people who are acting roles.

As you walk through life it's going to be very much like sitting in a theatre and seeing people playing roles. Your job is to look beyond the role they are playing.

Don't be an actor, be your divine Self.